For the King

Worcester, England 1264

To Eve,
All the best

Matthew Todd

For the King

First published in Great Britain in 2012 by Lux Ventus
Apartment 2/1, 162 St Andrews Road, Glasgow G41 1PG

matthew@mathew-todd.co.uk
www.matthew-todd.co.uk

ISBN 978-0-9572968-0-0

Publishing Consultancy: Zoesbooks Ltd, www.zoesbooks.co.uk

Illustrations: Dr. Graham Harris

Design: Afterhours Artwork, art@afterhours.myzen.co.uk

Printed by Berforts, www.berforts.co.uk

Contents

*Dedicated to David Grant, Benjamin Driver
and every child who has taught and inspired me.
Also to Dr Archie Ewing without whom this
would never have been possible.*

Chapter 1

Justin raced the river through the valley with all the joyful exuberance of a healthy and agile nine-year-old boy. His golden hair was still wet from a morning swim, and the dew soaked his bare feet as they sped through the long grass. The village became visible round the next bend: a mill, a little chapel, and a few dozen thatched cottages all huddled together like chickens in a nest.

Justin spotted a clump of wild flowers on the river bank and yanked them out as he ran past. Without too much damage to his bouquet, he managed to thrust it into his tunic where he hoped it would be safe until he arrived home. He did not slow his pace as the wet grass turned to a warm, well trodden earth beneath his feet. A strong smell of heavy horses and wood smoke clung permanently to the narrow pathways of the village that Justin loved as much as the pleasant bubble of the river and the creaking of the mill.

In less than a minute, Justin was bounding into the small room that he called home. It was cluttered with looms and cloth and other tools of a weaver's cottage, and his mother called to him as she sat pumping the pedal of her spinning wheel by the window,

"There is porridge in the pot, Justin dear. Could you dish it out and put on the table please?"

Justin walked over to her as he caught his breath,

"I picked these for you, Mother," he said, presenting the flowers to her with an endearing smile.

Oh how lovely!" gasped his mother, as she reverently accepted her gift with one hand and tried to embrace her son with the other. Justin dodged deftly and ran to the fireplace where he proceeded to ladle the porridge into two wooden bowls. He enquired as he did so:

"Mother, do I have to go to lessons? I don't really want to go today."

"What's the matter darling? Is someone being unkind to you?"

Justin turned up his eyes incredulously as he brought the bowls to the table. From what he had learned from his friends, this was the appropriate response to motherly concern!

"No mother, it's just that Father John makes me teach the older ones now. I don't mind teaching the little ones but ..."

His mother sat down at the table and took her bowl,

"Father John makes you teach the older ones?"

"Yes he does," frowned Justin standing on his stool and leaning his elbows on the table, "and I don't like it."

"Why not?"

"Well because" Justin paused and leaned forward confidentially, "you know those things you told me about... not bragging?"

His mother nodded seriously.

"Sometimes," said Justin with genuine remorse, "sometimes I forget, you see."

He leaned even further forward until he was almost lying on the table,

"I actually enjoy the lessons, you see, I think they're really interesting — well most of them anyway — like learning about the Romans and how to speak Latin and the history of the province and counting and writing and stuff. Anyway, when I teach the older ones they usually complain that it is boring or too hard and I sometimes forget not to brag and I say something like 'but this is easy isn't it', and then, then mother, they give me this face."

Justin contorted his handsome features into an envious scowl. His mother cleared her throat to hide a smile from her son, who was now staring eagerly and waiting for her answer to his problem,

"Well then, shall I speak with Father O'Brien about it?"

Justin nodded eagerly, as the young woman smiled at her son then commenced her breakfast,

"You're singing at evensong tonight so I'll talk to him after that. Now get off the table, eat your breakfast and go to your lessons!"

Father O'Brien was a cheerful old monk who, as well as taking the chapel choir, did much to hold the village together and strengthen the community. He often visited homes to hear the villagers' troubles and speak with them in his pleasant, sing-song voice and he was always at the forefront of events and celebrations. The entire village acknowledged that Father O'Brien was a man of true wisdom and integrity. Rarely was there a question that he did not know the answer to, and his gift for settling disputes of all kinds attracted well-deserved respect.

Justin took an innocent pleasure in almost everything in his young life, but nothing more so than singing with the chapel choir, directed by Father O'Brien. It filled him with awe to put on his cassock and surplice, process into the stone building and reverently bow to the altar; it thrilled him to sing praises to God and hear his voice reverberating around the stones as the singing filled the chapel.

As he walked to the choir rehearsal that evening, Justin allowed himself to slip into a pleasant day dream: he was in the city, inside the great cathedral that Father O'Brien had often described. The bishop heard him singing and asked him to join the choir to which he readily agreed. Suddenly, the cathedral was attacked by the evil barons. Everyone was too terrified to move, so Justin shouted orders to them, telling them to arm themselves and put archers in the cloisters. Then he drew his sword and fearlessly charged into the fray. But the dream took a turn that he did not expect: he was outnumbered and fighting to the death when a strong man dashed to his rescue and defeated the enemies. Justin was about to speak to this man when he was jerked back to reality by a loud voice from the open window of the busy village tavern:

"Well, if you want my opinion," said the blacksmith, placing his ale emphatically on the table, "whatever the reason may be, it's a darned sin for William to leave his lovely wife and that poor child of his."

"You're right enough there, Jim," the tanner's wife agreed, pulling up a chair, "not yet three years old that little boy was when William last showed up here. That unfortunate little soul will be growing up without a father's care and we all know well enough that can't be good for 'im at all. Why, if I think about my own growing up without…"

"Unless," the Mason said mysteriously, from the end of the table, making everyone lean backwards him in anticipation, "unless, he has deserted us. If he can betray his family why should he not betray his lord and Province too? Supposing he has been bribed by the barons and even now is helping to bring down Lord Athelstan and all of us!"

A hush fell over the table as they contemplated this chilling possibility. Suddenly, a tall monk from the monastery approached them irritably,

"What's all this gossip and slander I'm hearing?" he declared eying them all severely, "what right have you to judge a fellow countryman and what if Serena or little Justin were to hear of it? You should be ashamed of yourselves, all of you..."

Justin felt a strange, heavy sensation in the pit of his stomach as he left the scene and continued down the path. His father was a soldier defending the eastern border, but it was now almost eight years since he had been home. Whenever news of the rebellion, that had divided the country and was still fiercely fought in this corner of southern England, reached Evesham, the villagers would gather in anticipation. From the chapel gates in the town square, the Declaration of Exploits and the List of Slain Heroes, would be read out, bringing tales of bravery, courage and loss. But William, Justin's Father, was never read out in either.

Justin did not remember his father very clearly; he had a vague recollection of being held in strong arms, while a bearded face smiled proudly down at him, but nothing more. Nevertheless, Justin felt inexplicably sick with anger and sadness when people spoke ill of his father. Justin knew that his mother found William's absence very hard to bear and there were times when Justin felt quite guilty for not thinking of him more fondly and more often. But missing someone that you do not know is complicated and usually it did not enter the lively boy's mind. The villagers would sometimes mistake his dreaming as a form of silent grief for the father he had never met. They would ruffle his hair and say something like "he will come back some day, you'll see". Justin liked it when people said that, he was not sure if he believed it, but he loved to hear it anyway.

Justin was regularly late for choir rehearsal, but his excuses were always so fantastical that they had earned him an unofficial indulgence for tardiness. As he stumbled through the chapel door, his cassock still under his arm, the choir turned towards him smiling in anticipation of some wild excuse and Father O'Brien folded his arms in mock severity as he enquired,

"Well Justin, what's the story this time?"

Justin tried to smile but found that he could not. He tried to think of one of his best excuses but, when his lips parted, a subdued 'sorry' was all that emerged. The dozen or so boys and four men of the choir lost interest immediately but Father O'Brien raised an enquiring eyebrow to the young chorister. Justin managed to force a smile and no more was said.

The music quickly healed Justin's spirits and all thoughts of his father vanished from his mind as he sang with all his body, mind and soul. It was a beautiful evensong and a rare atmosphere of peace and calm filled the chapel. As the service ended, Justin ran out into the fading sunlight, with his cassock under his arm, and met his mother walking towards the chapel,

"Go home and get a fire going, Justin," she whispered, "I'll be back when I've spoken with Father O'Brien."

An early autumn breeze set the tallow candles flickering as the door closed. Justin's mother approached the old monk as he was clearing the chant sheets from the choir stalls,

"Father, might I speak with you for a moment?"

Father O'Brien dumped the pile of expensive parchment on the lectern and smiled,

"About Justin?"

"Yes, about Justin."

They sat on a pew in the silent, stone building, Father O'Brien looked thoughtfully at the women in front of him, whom he had known since she was a young girl. Serena possessed the same innocent, endearing charm as her son, as well as a unique elegance and grace in her manner and appearance. She seemed so happy and carefree, yet a deep mystery glimmered in her eyes like a crescent moon. She tried, rather unsuccessfully, to hide her eagerness as she spoke,

"Father, I'm sure you know what I'm going to say. I know mothers tend to exaggerate their children's talents but I'm not the only one who has noticed that Justin ..."

"Is exceptional?"

Serena sighed and lifted her eyes to meet Father O'Brien's,

"Yes. I don't want him to grow up without fulfilling his potential, Father, but there is nothing for him here. I want to help him, but what can I do?"

Father O'Brien leaned forward, making direct eye contact in his honest way,

"Serena, there is something that I have been meaning to ask you for some time but I was not sure, until now, if the time was right: would Justin consider continuing his education with myself and the Brothers in the monastery?"

Serena was momentarily stunned by the offer, when she realised that it was a serious proposal her face broke into a beaming smile,

"There is no power in the world that could stop him! It would be his wildest dream come true, Father."

"Excellent. He can learn to read and write, we'll teach him how to ride and how to hunt and introduce him to philosophy and history. Father John tells me he works faster than the others in the schoolroom so it's only fair to offer him the opportunities that he deserves."

Serena smiled sincerely,

"It is so good of you to offer this, Father. I know it is what Justin wants and it is what William would want too." Her smile slowly faded, "Will he stay in the monastery? How often will I see him?"

"Oh, as often as you like, my dear," said Father O'Brien warmly. "For the first while we can take him home every evening before supper and he can sleep in his own bed. It's not much more than a fifteen-minute ride to the monastery when you know the way as well as I do."

Serena gazed with gratitude at the cheerful monk,

"Why are you doing this, Father?"

"Three reasons really," said the old man, with a twinkle in his eye, "First, because it's the best thing for the boy, secondly, because the monastery could do with someone to shake them up and it's great for them to have someone to teach their skills to, but, most importantly…" he suddenly turned very serious,

"Serena, there are some children that possess a very specific and precious quality. I call it puerilis servitus – childlike servitude. It is the duty and privilege of my Order to encourage and nurture every child who possesses puerilis servitus and I am almost certain that Justin is one of them."

"What makes you think so, Father?" asked Serena in a low voice.

"You get to know the signs with experience," said Father O'Brien nodding to himself. "They are often highly intelligent, filled with a love of life, and not easily affected by peer pressure. They can somehow remain contented when everyone else is discontented; or be thoughtful when everyone else is being thoughtless. They do not seem to notice that they are different and, if they do, it does not worry them. You see, Serena, most people are controlled by their natural instincts, but these few are controlled by something deeper. It inspires them from within and gives them sensitivity for others and a love of sharing everything they have. God grants us just a few of these children in every generation, but too often they are pulled down by a world that does not understand them or their gift. That is why we must protect them."

"I'm not sure I fully understand, Father," said Serena quietly.

Father O'Brien leaned back,

"I'm afraid you can't fully understand: you are his mother and he is your son. But what you need to know is that Justin is a child who, if he stays strong, can change the world by simply being himself. He is everything a boy should be and he deserves the chance to become everything a man should be."

Father O'Brien stood up,

"It's a cold, dark night. Come, I'll walk you home."

Serena took the old monk's arm and listened contentedly to his cheerful conversation as they walked along together,

"Did I ever tell you, Serena, about the time when Justin was late for choir practice for the third time in a row? It was last month if I remember, I think he must talk to the blacksmith's little girl before he comes in, but anyway, he dashed into the chapel out of breath with his cassock in a mess as usual and I asked 'what's the story this time?' He answered simply that 'he was singing to a poor orphan'. 'I don't think that's true?' I said. He looked at me rather worried and said 'but it is' then added 'I mean she's not an orphan and I don't think she's poor and I wasn't singing to her but other than that it's true!' Well that set the boys and the men into a riot of hilarity and I couldn't for the life of me be sure if he knew what they were laughing at!"

"Oh, I dare say he did," smiled Serena, "in nine years he's learned how to exploit an innocent face if nothing else!"

They talked and laughed their way to the door of Serena's home,

"Won't you come in for a while, Father?"

"I'd love to while I get my strength back. Then I'll wander back to the monastery; I enjoy an evening stroll up the hill."

Justin had the fire blazing and was throwing on logs when they entered the little house. Straw mattresses lay in the corner, out of the way of the looms and cloth that filled most of the room. As Father O'Brien walked in behind his mother, Justin greeted him warmly, he was never shy; having been shown nothing but love and kindness all his life, he knew no fear and had no reason to be afraid of anyone. He glowed with pleasure when he was told of the plans for his training. The monastery had captured his imagination and for years he had longed to find out what lay behind its high stone wall.

Serena had not felt so peaceful for a long time, there was something about Father O'Brien that radiated a strange feeling of calm and comfort and even security; she watched with fascination as he spoke to her son. Justin asked lots of sensible questions, but also many ridiculous ones, yet the wise monk answered them all without a hint of hesitation and not once was there anything remotely patronising in his tone. He spoke to Justin as an equal, but always using vocabulary that he would understand. If Justin said something, as he often did, which was too naive or amusing to be answered with anything but laughter, Father O'Brien would effortlessly turn the joke on himself and Justin's laughter was soon ringing with their own.

When the fire had sunk to a warm ember and Justin had fallen asleep in front of it, Father O'Brien stood up and prepared to leave. Serena waited until he had put on his long cloak then opened the door for him,

"I don't know how to thank you, Father," she said with lowered eyes.

"Good! Your thanks on top of the greatest pleasure I have ever allowed myself might just be too much to bear!"

"I feel sure I can trust you and all the brothers."

"Trust us? Oh yes, you can trust us, my dear, though I can't vouch for any other monastery, abbey or cathedral in England. The war has made us all suspicious, as we try to discover who is for the king or the rebel barons, but we must never give in to the temptation to judge our friends in fear."

Serena delayed the parting, she opened her mouth to speak but a quavering sigh was all that emerged. Father O'Brien looked at her for a few moments; there was a restrained desperation in her eyes that was struggling to escape. He took her hand in his and said gently,

"What is troubling you, my dear? You know that you can tell me."

Serena's hand was trembling,

"I wish I could, Father. Someday I will."

Chapter 2

Serena was not disturbed to wake up in the morning and find Justin's bed empty. He often started his day with a run on the hillside or, if the weather was fine, even a swim in the river and was always back in time for breakfast along with a healthy appetite! Today was no exception and he bounded into the little room just as the porridge was being ladled into the wooden bowls on the table. He ran to Serena and thrust another fistful of flowers at her (which also included a good deal of fresh grass!) and attacked his breakfast without waiting to hear her exclamation of delight. The flowers were carefully placed in an earthenware bowl by the window and the slightly withered previous occupants of the bowl were thrown onto the fire. When Justin had demolished two and a half bowls of porridge, he paused briefly and looked up,

"When am I going to the monastery, Mother?" he asked as if suddenly remembering that the previous night had not been a dream.

"This morning, Justin," answered his mother with a smile, "I am to bring you up as soon as you're ready."

"Oh, you don't need to come," said Justin quickly as if a parental presence would be entirely inappropriate. But then, checking his tone added, "Unless you want to."

At first, Serena was sure that she would have to come for his first day at least. But the more she thought about it, the more she was inclined to think that her presence would do nothing but dilute the experience for her son. The truth of the matter was: Justin needed a male influence. For most of his life he had known no other care than that of a woman, and a kind, gentle woman at that. His own compassionate heart had been nurtured and released, but within Justin there was also an adventurer's spirit which she could neither control nor set free. It grew stronger as he matured and Serena knew that this spirit required a care she could not give.

"Will you be alright walking up there by yourself?" she asked with no doubt as to what the answer would be.

Justin merely made a heroic gesture which was supposed to indicate that walking up a hill to one's destiny was something which, against all adversity, had to be done alone.

When he had finished his breakfast and packed anything he supposed might be needed into a sack which he carried over his back, he headed up the hill without a backwards glance.

It was a good hour's walk to the Monastery for a nine-year-old boy, but a very pleasant journey. The autumn leaves were rustling through the cool air and a gentle midday sun bathed the hillside in a comforting orange glow. From the top of the hill, it seemed that half the province was visible and Justin loved to stare wistfully into the eastern horizon and imagine the epic battles that were taking place at that moment. All children were taught the importance of the brave men on the border who were defending them and their homes and were told to give thanks for them in their prayers and remember them at all times, but none, of course, had ever met one. In some ways this made it hard to appreciate but, on the other hand, it let imagination fill the place of experience which held far greater potential. He had heard people whisper about the war when they thought there were no children near, but he could never catch enough to make sense of the rumours. Every time a grown up saw him or one of his friends listening they would clumsily change the subject and assume an exaggerated grin until the child eventually left in frustration.

On arriving at the gates of the monastery, Justin's courage almost failed him, it seemed unlikely that anything other than something huge and ominous could be behind those imposing, studded doors. The doubt was momentary however, and, with a final glance around him and a little shudder, Justin thudded three times on the massive oak doors with all his might.

Unfortunately, his best efforts produced little more than a dull thud on the solid timber and the knocks were unanswered. Justin was left shivering in the chilly wind and slightly doubtful as to his next move. He searched for a knocker, but the doors had nothing except a huge keyhole which was too high for him to peek into. He tried shouting but, after one half hearted attempt, found that this too had little effect and was not much in the mood to try again.

Eventually, he huddled against the door and sat and waited. There was a cold wind up on the hill and his cape and sack were his only shelter, he soon fell to dreamy contemplation of the eastern border as he watched the sun creep towards the western horizon where it would eventually sink out of sight. Presently, Justin forgot where he was and why he was there and let his thoughts wander where they pleased while he shivered in the waning afternoon.

His imagination led him back to the cathedral: the man who had rescued Justin from the barons was standing with his back to him, silhouetted against a stained glass window. There now was something frightening and imposing about him which Justin had not noticed before. He still desperately wanted to speak to the man but was not sure if he dared. He crept up quietly and opened his mouth, but nothing came out. The man turned round...

Justin was jerked back into reality as the door at his back suddenly swung open and he heard an exclamation of surprise, as a tall, robed man almost tripped over him. Before Justin could turn round he had been hauled to his feet by a strong arm and swung round to meet a stern face eyeing him suspiciously,

"What are you doing here?" asked the man in a deep bass that was void of all emotion.

Through a combination of cold and fear, Justin completely lost his voice. He tried to speak but all that came out was a rasping whisper. The monk looked him up and down,

"Come on now, you are trespassing and we cannot have that. What is in the sack?" The monk suddenly shouted, "Can you speak?"

Justin nodded and coughed. No-one had ever spoken to him so harshly before and it terrified him. He swallowed,

"I'm here... to see Father...", he managed to rasp.

"Father? I guarantee your father does not live here."

Justin felt a strong desire to turn around and run away, but at that moment he heard a kind, familiar voice coming up behind him,

"Oh Justin, my boy! I thought you had got lost. I called at your home and your mother said you had walked up alone."

Justin was so relieved that he turned, ran to Father O'Brien and hugged him tightly. The old monk laughed and held the boy steady with a strong arm,

"Now, my poor child, why did you not come in the side door like I told you? I had no idea you were lying outside the portal."

He picked up Justin's sack and guided the shivering boy along the stone passageway and into a huge warm hall with a great wooden banqueting table in the centre and a roaring fire at the far end.

"Who is the man that was shouting at me, Father?" said Justin glancing around nervously.

"That was Brother Oswald, my boy. He was heading out the main door for some fire-wood."

"He was scary."

"Oh, I don't think he means to be. He just has a bit of a dry sense of humour. And then there is the 'very strict rule'. Brother Oswald is very strict about the very strict rule. And, of course, he does not like children very much..." Father O'Brien thought for a moment then muttered grimly, "In all honesty, Brother Oswald must have given you a bad impression of the monastery. But never mind, my boy, the good news is you're just in time for dinner."

Presently, numerous monks began to flock in with various contributions of vegetables, drink and even meat to add to the table. Justin eyed the intimidating, robed men suspiciously at first, and if one smiled pleasantly at him he first looked to Father O'Brien, as if seeking confirmation that this individual was genuine before he would return the smile.

Soon, however, the monks where all seated along the table and talking to each other in such a surprisingly friendly manner that Justin could hardly prevent himself from being swept along in the general merriment. Brother Oswald presently arrived and, seeing Justin, immediately approached him. Justin involuntarily clung to Father O'Brien on seeing the imposing figure, but Brother Oswald came up and laid a hand on the boy's shoulder,

"I apologise for my harsh manner, Justin. It is a very strict rule that no-one may enter the monastery without express permission so I had no choice but to keep you outside until I had confirmed your identity."

Father O'Brien laughed and said, "I do believe, in future, Brother Oswald, that I shall make shivering children lying on the doorstep an exception to the 'very strict rule'."

"Yes, Father," said Brother Oswald with something that could have been his undemonstrative equivalent of a smile.

When the table was settled to a degree, Father O'Brien stood up and said, in a clear voice, 'a Deo gratias tibi' to which the rest replied 'Deo gratias'. With that, the food was unceremoniously attacked and the room became a place of much appreciated consumption.

Justin stared up at Father O'Brien open mouthed; it took a few moments for the monk to notice, since the food in front of him demanded much of his attention, but he eventually glanced at Justin and saw his somewhat over-awed expression,

"Is everything alright, my boy?"

Justin closed his mouth and nodded. Then opened it again to ask quietly,

"Are you in charge of this whole place?"

Father O'Brien nodded and grinned like a cheeky child,

"Oh yes, are you surprised, my boy?"

Justin smiled, slowly, he began to relax a little and his spirits returned with his appetite. After eating some food and listening to the hearty conversations, he was soon laughing, joking and eating as much as any of the other diners.

Once the food was gone, the conversations became even more lively as the monks attempted to make Justin laugh and feel at ease, then Father O'Brien stood up and gave several very loud claps which presently brought silence to the hall. After listening to the crackling of the fire for a few seconds the monk addressed the assembly:

"Brothers, thank you all for a wonderful meal and a very pleasant evening. Now get back to work and, for goodness sake, look busy because I'm going to be bringing our young novice round for a tour of our monastery. Right now, move."

Swiftly and silently the monks dispersed, seamlessly clearing the table as they did so. Justin looked up at Father O'Brien with admiration; the choir didn't obey him so well. Justin could never have imagined what a huge and powerful place the monastery was and yet the man he had known all his life was in charge of it...

The boy's energy had been completely revitalised and he commenced his tour of the magnificent building with wide-eyed wonder. The first room outside the great hall was smaller but even grander. The walls and floors were strewn with tapestries and paintings, which numerous monks were working on or swiftly preparing to do so.

"This is the work room. We make these things to sell and trade mostly and, believe me, there's a lot to be made from it!"

"Just as well!" laughed a monk from the floor below with a large needle between his teeth.

Justin looked down at the tapestry the monk was working on and caught his breath. The picture was almost finished: it showed a man in armour standing on a rock with crowds of people reaching out to him. One hand was mail-clad and held a huge sword pointing straight into the sky; the other, bare, hand was stretched towards the crowds. The face of tiny threads stared steadily out of the tapestry; one eye was not yet complete and Justin watched in fascination as, while the monk worked, a second eye of thread began to gaze fixedly at him.

"This one is valuable," grinned the monk, "it's a commission for Lord Athelstan himself. This is a picture of him standing on the rock of faith with a hand of compassion for his subjects and a hand of iron for his enemies."

This was said quite casually, assuming Justin would not understand or be very interested. But the boy knelt beside the work of art in silence and gazed steadily at it for several minutes. Slowly and reverently, he stretched out a hand and gently touched the silken-thread broadsword. He said in almost a whisper,

"It's beautiful. Lord Athelstan must be a very good man to be given this."

"He is a good man, thanks be to God," said Father O'Brien glancing up. "We should be grateful for that."

The next room Justin was shown was the writing room, where several desks were surrounded by piles of parchments and monks were diligently writing. Again, Justin was fascinated by the ornate lettering and the tireless love and attention that went in to creating it.

"What are they writing, Father?" he whispered.

"Most of them are copying the Bible in Latin," he answered in a low voice, "some are writing or copying documents of state and some are writing letters."

"I can read Latin I think: I can do all the lessons Father John gives me."

"And you have all your life to read and improve," smiled Father O'Brien. "We'll head to the chapel now; it's nearly time for evensong."

On the way, Justin noticed a solid, studded door set deep into a large protruding area of wall.

"Where does that go?" he whispered.
"Oh that's the door to the tower. It's a safe place to go in emergencies."

"What kind of emergency?"

"Oh any kind, or just when you need a bit of peace and quiet and a good view."

Justin clicked up the latch with his thumb and tried to push the door open; it did not move.

"Can I go in it?"

"It's all locked up but I'll show you it someday."

All thoughts of the mysterious tower vanished from Justin's mind as he heard the sound of singing echoing along the stone corridor from the chapel. A Latin chant was followed by a burst of song in perfect polyphony which filled not just the chapel but, seemingly, the whole monastery with a torrent of heavenly harmony. Justin had never heard anything like it in his life. He had thought the choir he sang with down in the village had been the most amazing sound in the world, but now he found himself surrounded by music which pierced his heart and filled him with awe. Following Father O'Brien into the candle-lit, scented, stone room, Justin sat completely captivated until the song finished and the world became real once more.

He found the spoken liturgy quite boring, because it was in Latin and he did not understand it as well as he thought he did. Justin did not want to ask Father O'Brien what was they were saying, because the other monks seemed quite strict about not talking in the chapel.

The final song was a minor piece starting with a lone voice and building up to eight interweaving parts. Again he sat in silent fascination, as Father O'Brien whispered in his ear that the words meant 'grant us peace' and suddenly it seemed as if the music came to life. He could hear the ardent plea raised to Heaven and he felt every bit of the passion with which it was being sung. Closing his eyes, he let it fill his mind as the world became a sea of sacred music. When he vaguely became aware that the music had stopped and opened his eyes, he saw an empty chapel. Father O'Brien stood at the door beckoning to him with a smile.

"Did you fall asleep?" asked Father O'Brien when they were back out in the corridor.

"I don't think so, though my eyes feel a little bit heavy," answered Justin. "I was just listening, it was so lovely…"

"Yes it must have been," smiled Father O'Brien. "You know, most boys your age would find that sort of ecclesiastical music quite dull."

Justin blinked and stared thoughtfully back into the chapel,

"Then they can't be listening. I don't think most people really listen to anything at all."

Father O'Brien led the boy back along the corridor,

"I believe you are right, my boy. Most people think they do not have time to listen, but in fact they are just afraid of what they might hear. Look at what can be achieved when people put themselves to one side and work for God and for others. There are not many places like this in the world, not even in other monasteries and abbeys. Corruption creeps in, but not here, the brothers never lose sight of their goal."

They turned out of a small side door that led to the courtyard. Father O'Brien took a lantern from the stand by the door,

"Anyway, it is dark, we had better get you home."

"Yes, Mother will be worried if I'm not back soon."
"Oh, we'll have you back in no time. The last thing you have to see is the stables, Samson hasn't had his exercise today and he will be delighted to take you down the hill."

The stables were round the back of the monastery and sheltered dozens of huge, elegant horses. All stood at least twice as tall as Justin and he felt quite nervous as they neighed and snorted from their stalls and the strange, strong, 'stable' smell filled his nostrils. Father O'Brien greeted the horses by name as he walked past and told Justin confidentially that the monastery's horses were bred for Lord Athelstan's personal guard. Giving Justin the lantern to hold, he walked into one stall and emerged leading a huge black stallion,

"Samson is being trained for Lord Athelstan himself, but he's still a bit too touchy. It's probably not worth confusing the poor beast by saddling him up at this late hour; we'll just use a halter and ride bareback."

Justin was trembling, half with fear, half with excitement, as he was lifted onto the huge animal. The great broad back was twice the size of anything he had ever ridden before and it felt extremely precarious. Sitting there, his head was as high as it would be if he had been standing on a tall man's shoulders.

Father O'Brien grabbed a handful of mane and swung himself up in front of Justin. Without being prompted, Samson began to walk out of the gate. Justin felt sure he was going to fall off as he felt his seat shifting when the huge horse's muscles pulsated up and down, so he clung tightly to the rider in front.

"Relax, boy," laughed Father O'Brien. "Try to move with the horse… that's it. Become one with your steed. Do you want to go a bit faster?"

Justin nodded, unaware that this could not be seen by the person in front.

"Do you want to go a bit faster?" repeated Father O'Brien louder.
"Yes," shouted Justin to make himself heard. However, this was interpreted by the rider as an exuberant cry for more speed so, very soon, horse, man and boy were hurtling down the hill at a brisk canter.

Initially, Justin panicked as the ground became a blur and the motion of the horse became like riding a stormy ocean. He instantly tensed up but, after further orders to relax, found himself naturally moving with the rhythm of the horse and, presently, he began to enjoy the experience immensely.

They soon clattered into the village and arrived safely at Justin's home where a pleasant orange glow emerged from between the shutters. Justin was lifted down gently and set, slightly unsteadily, on his feet again.

"Now have a good sleep and say hello to your mother for me. Will I see you tomorrow?"

Justin nodded, and ran inside smiling.

Father O'Brien smiled also. He was about to mount Samson and canter back up the hill when Serena dashed out from the house,

"Father, I just wanted to thank you for doing this."

Even in the dim light, Father O'Brien could see that Serena had been crying. Her eyes were red and her golden hair was tangled. He took her trembling hand,

"Are you unwell, my dear?" he asked in a low voice.

Serena tried to force a smile,

"I'm fine, Father," she said hoarsely. "Justin being away for the whole day brought it all back to me, that's all. I don't want my son to see me like this. I will be myself in a moment."

Father O'Brien held her hand tightly,

"You still miss William?"

Serena nodded and gritted her teeth,

"I miss him... so much..."

Father O'Brien could not think what to say, this time, he did not have the answer.

Chapter 3

Justin went to the monastery every day except Sundays. The brothers trained him in all their arts and he swiftly and eagerly learnt everything. Father O'Brien rode him home every day on Samson and, if the weather was bad, he would often pick him up at his home.

Serena noted her son's progress with delight. She was an intelligent woman and knew that her son deserved an education that neither she nor the village could give him alone. She could see Justin's potential just as Father O'Brien had seen it and knew in her heart that the boy's future was not in the village and, in all probability, was not with her. So, one Sunday night after evensong, on the day before Justin's tenth birthday, she brought her request to Father O'Brien,

"Father, I was wondering if I might speak to you."

Father O'Brien sat promptly in a pew laughing,

"About Justin?"

"Yes," laughed Serena "what else!"

Soon they were sitting in the cool chapel just as they had done several weeks before. As Serena spoke, she did not attempt to hide the eagerness in her voice.

"Father, how good is Justin? His singing I mean. Is he good enough to go to the city and sing in the cathedral?"

Father O'Brien looked at her expressionlessly,

"Yes, if he auditioned I dare say he would be successful, but there is no guarantee."

Serena paused in thought then said quietly,

"I want him to have the success he deserves. They won't take him if he is much older and I need to know that I have given him every chance."

Father O'Brien spoke in a low, careful tone,

"You know that the city folk don't understand sensitive boys like Justin, Serena. They would chew him up and spit him out. If it is the war you are concerned about then I must tell you that the barons will march straight for the city if they invade."

There was a determination in Serena's voice,

"It is not the war I am worried about, Father. If Justin grows up in the village, this province will never appreciate his qualities; never take him seriously; never... never realise how much they need him."

Father O'Brien continued to stare steadily into her face,

"But what about you, my dear, you need him too."

Serena could not answer that and there was a long silence which Father O'Brien broke with a heavy sigh,

"Serena, you are the most selfless, humble woman I have ever met. It so happens that I have been looking for a possible employment for your son for some time now. What you say about the city is true and if Justin is to be successful there he would need an early start. There is a post in the castle for a boy to act as Lord Athelstan's personal page which Justin might fill. His Lordship has many problems on his mind and he himself expressed the desire for a young boy to wait on him and sing for him on occasion. He expressly asked for a boy unconnected with the city. Justin would be trained at the cathedral of course and could sing there too if he wanted; he would stay in the choir school with the other choristers. I have said nothing so far to either party: the decision is yours."

There was another stunned silence then Serena asked anxiously,

"Do you know Lord Athelstan, has he asked you about Justin?"

"I have never met him in person, but I have it on good authority that he is an excellent man. Now Serena, I know you want the best for your son, but I must tell you that if you are not happy, Justin will never be. What will you do without him?"

A faraway look entered the young woman's eyes,

"I am happy, Father, and nothing would make me happier than knowing that Justin is fulfilling his destiny. It is what his father would have wanted."

"Serena, forgive me for my bluntness but I should like to know: do you know where William is."

Serena jumped visibly at the mention of her husband's name and answered softly,

"I know he is alive for certain. I know he is still faithful because I trust him."

"But you must hear how the villagers talk. It will hurt little Justin soon. It is bad enough that he must live fatherless without him growing up to believe that his father is a traitor."

Suddenly, Serena's voice had a defiant edge,

"I cannot say how I know, but my husband is not a traitor."

Father O'Brien knew he had said too much, but he pushed one final question,

"Why can't you say how you know?"

Serena began to look uncomfortable and said firmly,

"Because of a promise. A promise that I cannot break. Not even to you."

Father O'Brien smiled,

"Well in that case, my dear, I have nothing more to say. I will make the necessary arrangements. It will take some time, so Justin will be with us for a few months yet. I promise to look after Justin's future, but you must promise to look after your own."

Serena smiled and nodded.

"Thank you, Father, I promise and I will be happy now. God bless you."

The two then walked slowly out of the chapel and made their way to Serena's home where her son had already began to light the fire. Father O'Brien was asked to stay and gladly accepted once again. In truth he was keen to see how Justin would react to the news of his planned employment.

"Justin," said Serena, moving to sit on the floor beside her son, who was lying with his hands on his chin and staring into the fire.

"Do you remember we spoke a while ago about cathedrals and the big city?"

Justin turned to her eagerly, the firelight dancing in his bright eyes. Serena paused for a moment then continued,

"Would you like to go to the city and be a choirboy there?"

Justin's face became a picture of excitement and enthusiasm,

"You mean, sing in the cathedral! Really?"

"Father O'Brien has found you a position with Lord Athelstan. You will be singing for him sometimes and acting as his page. The choir school will be your home and if you want you can sing in the cathedral too."

Justin could hardly speak for excitement and it took several minutes before he was calm enough to be given the details of his new employment.

When Justin was finally in bed and making a good enough impression of being asleep, Father O'Brien turned to Serena, and asked seriously,

"Now then, there are certain things he will have to know before he leaves. Have you ever told him about... the state of the province?"

Serena looked slightly shocked and shook her head. Father O'Brien added hastily,

"No, of course not. That was tactless of me. Would you like me to explain it to him?"

"Yes Father."

"Then I will. Tomorrow. You know Serena; you could go to the city too."

Serena paused and looked away,

"I think I must stay here, Father."

"Why?"

Father O'Brien could tell that she was longing to tell him but she said nothing so he stood up and took his cloak,

"I am sorry my dear, I will never ask you again."

The next day, Justin arrived at the great monastery with his usual energy and enthusiasm. Father O'Brien met him with a more subdued demeanour than usual, but still smiled at him warmly. The old monk spoke to the boy as they walked along the long, cool corridor towards the chapel,

"Justin, my boy, how much do you know about our province? You know there is a war on don't you?"

Justin spoke casually, concentrating on his feet on the smooth, stone floor more than what he was saying,

"Of course, my father is fighting on the border and we all must send the soldiers food and clothes to keep them going and remember them in our prayers."

Father O'Brien stopped at the mysterious, studded door and slowly unlocked it,

"Would you like to see the tower, Justin?"

Justin nodded eagerly and they made their way up a spiral staircase, dimly lit by slits in the walls that let slender beams of daylight illuminate the way. The steps were so steep that Justin had to climb them one at a time with Father O'Brien walking patiently behind him, it seemed like a long time before they finally reached the top. A huge oak door blocked the way, but it was not locked and swung open when Justin gave it a push. Inside, it was pitch black, the windows were blocked by heavy shutters and the room was cold and damp. Father O'Brien struck some tinder to light a torch beside the doorway and instantly the place was illuminated with an orange glow.

Justin gasped, the room was much bigger than he had thought it would be and it was filled with shining weapons and armour. A large round table stood in the centre, littered with maps and documents, Father O'Brien walked towards it and bent over one of the maps with a sombre expression. Justin tried to peek over and the monk lifted him onto the table so could see,

"This is a map of Britain as far as we know it, and this —" he pointed to a small area on the map "this is our province under the rule of Lord Athelstan."

Justin peered curiously at it, noting with pleasure the smell of the old parchment, and was surprised at how small the province looked in a corner of southern Britain,

"But I thought our province was huge."

"It is," said Father O'Brien, "but Britain is much bigger. Our town is just here, near the south-eastern border of the province. Do you know what the war is about?"

"Something to do with Montfort and some bad barons."

Father O'Brien smiled very slightly:

"More or less. But they are not all bad barons. Some are bad, some are greedy, others are cowards but many are just disillusioned. They are following Simon de Montfort in his attempt to supplant King Henry the Third and dissolve the monarchy. They call themselves the Baron's Alliance."

Justin swung his legs and tried to understand how this complicated lesson relevant to him,

"Mother said that you used to know King Henry, Father?"

Father O'Brien gazed at the table, remembering silently,

"I knew him. I was present at his coronation and with him as he grew up. He was younger than you when he became king, Justin: not even ten years old. It had to be conducted in a hurry so it was a simple affair. The bishop placed a band of gold on his head and crowned him Henry the Third of England. I was one of his tutors teaching him Latin and music. He was a keen learner and loved art and architecture. We had such hopes for him; for what he would achieve. He was always pious and gentle mannered and some saw this as a weakness. People he should have been able to trust took advantage of him and manipulated his words. I did everything I could but, as the years went on, they drove us out one by one and, now, they have betrayed the king. He was too weak, too weak for this wicked world."

Justin sat quietly on the table studying the map. He noticed that all the provinces in the south, except their own, were marked with the same symbol. For some reason, this was strangely intimidating and he dreaded to voice the question that he feared he could guess the answer to,

"Father, are we... safe here?"

Father O'Brien sighed and put a gentle hand on the boy's shoulder. After a long silence he said quietly,

"Justin, my boy, it is time for you to know something about our province. Do not tell this to any of your friends. You must promise to listen carefully and to be brave."

Justin's heart thumped painfully against his chest. He felt small and helpless,

"I promise, Father."

34

Father O'Brien took a deep breath and avoided eye-contact with the boy,

"After the king was betrayed there was civil war in the land: the Baron's Alliance against us - the Loyalists. We lost the war and Henry was imprisoned by Montfort and the Baron's Alliance. Our province is the last in the south of England that is still loyal to the crown. We are surrounded by enemies and if they invade we do not have the strength to repel them. It may be months, it may be years, but life as we know it will not go on forever."

There was a long silence in which Justin started to tremble. His voice emerged thin and quavering,

"But why does it matter so much? Is Montfort a really bad man? Couldn't we just pretend that we were on his side and stop fighting?"

"If only it were that simple, Justin. Montfort is not a bad man. Many people have been inspired by him and his preaching of freedom and equality but a desire for power overcame him, and he broke his oath of obedience to the king. We must never give in to such desires. Besides, even if Lord Athelstan surrendered our province now, all Loyalists would be executed, and if the armies of the Baron's Alliance reach the city they will pillage it no matter what the terms are. They have been trying to take this province for years."

Justin stared desperately up at Father O'Brien in the flickering light,

"But if the king has been captured then it is all over. Why don't we just surrender?"

Father O'Brien leaned closer and looked straight into the boy's fearful eyes,

"Because that is weakness, Justin, and we must be strong. No-one should ever make a promise that they cannot keep. Not Montfort, not me and not you."

An edge of panic entered Justin's young voice,

"But why do we have to fight? Why won't they leave us alone?"

Father O'Brien gravely held the boy steady,

"Just calm down, Justin. It's alright."

Justin struggled and screamed,

"It's not alright! Why do people always say it's alright when it's not! We're all going to die: is that alright!"

Father O'Brien held the panicking child firmly and shouted in a voice that echoed round the room,

"Justin, listen to me!"

Justin instantly fell silent, this was the first time he had never heard Father O'Brien shout. It sounded very different to his soothing speaking voice and revealed a suppressed power and authority that the boy had never seen before. The monk looked him directly in the eye and said quietly, but firmly,

"It is not all hopeless, Justin. The fighting has been going on for years and the Baron's Alliance might soon decide that there are better things for them to waste their soldiers and resources on than conquering an indomitable province which is of little threat to them. They have the northern provinces to deal with. But whatever happens, we must be strong and stand up for what we believe, just as hundreds of people including your own father have been doing for years."

Father O'Brien gently caught the trembling boy as he burst into tears and buried his face in the monk's habit. Justin sobbed quietly for about five minutes then stopped and lay breathing heavily.

"I'm sorry, Father," he said in a muffled, husky voice.

"For despairing or for crying?" said Father O'Brien. "You only need to be sorry for something you have done wrong, my boy. Despairing does not help anyone, but there is nothing wrong with letting your feelings out before they get the better of you. That way you can deal with them and move on."

"Grown-up people don't cry," sniffed Justin.

"Not enough perhaps. They tend to find other ways of dealing with their emotions: starting wars is a favourite!"

"Mother never cries."

Father O'Brien smiled and gave Justin's shoulder a comforting squeeze,

"You would be surprised, my boy. Do you think my Henry never cried when he was your age? Even a king needs to cry sometimes. Anyway, I'm sure you feel better now, don't you?"

Justin nodded. He took a deep breath,

"Father, I'm not a child any more. From now on, I want to be strong. Strong like you and the Brothers."

Father O'Brien smiled,

"Believe it or not, my little Henry said the same thing to me one day. Do you know what I told him?"

Justin shook his head.

"Well he was meant to be studying his Latin at the time so I told him: 'qui non dat quod habet non accipit ille quod optat', which means 'he who does not give what he has will not gain what he wants.' He liked it so much he declared it to be his royal motto."

Then, the monk walked over to a wooden casket and took from it a short sword in an ornate scabbard,

"You are ten years old today," he smiled, "here is a gift from me and all the Brothers. The king's personal motto is inscribed on it. You have so much to give, Justin, and someday you will gain what you want."

All thoughts of wars and kings flew from Justin's head as he received his gift. His eyes shone with excitement as he examined it all over. Drawing it from the scabbard, he saw it was as long as his arm, but light enough for him to swing with reasonable ease thanks to its perfect balance. Father O'Brien looked on with satisfaction,

"You can play with it as much as you like, it is not sharp. We've sewn a piece of flint into the belt so you can sharpen it yourself if there is ever the need."

He added grimly, "It might be soon."

Then, he drew a short sword from a nearby basket,

"So let's teach you to use that thing."

Justin noted the casual, practised ease with which Father O'Brien handled his weapon. It soon became clear that the monk was adept and must have spent a considerable amount of his life with a sword in his hand. He had already taught Justin to ride a horse and shoot a bow, but they had seemed natural skills to have. Justin could not help wondering how Father O'Brien had acquired this talent.

They started with a figure-of-eight movement to get the feel of the balance of the weapon, and then they moved on to foot-work and parrying blows. Justin learned quickly though he had never used a blade before. There was something about the way that Father O'Brien spoke to him that told Justin that he was moving out of the realms of his previous training: he was learning something that, for once, everyone hoped he would never have to use.

After the novice had been disarmed several times Father O'Brien said,

"Alright, that is enough for now Justin. Let's see what you can do with your hands. It works in the same way except that you have less reach and everything moves a good deal faster. Now, I'm trusting you not to use this on any of your friends!"

Again, Justin grasped the basics almost immediately and Father O'Brien taught him as eagerly as the boy learned.

"Where did you learn all this, Father?" asked Justin gazing up at his teacher in awe.

"We are an order of warrior monks, Justin. All the Brothers are highly trained so that they can defend the weak and fight injustice. I am afraid to say that basic combat skills are now essential."

Father O'Brien picked up Justin's sword from the floor and, holding it carefully by the blade, presented it to the boy. As Justin closed his fingers around the hilt the monk covered the boy's hand with his own and knelt in front of him,

"Never use this or any other weapon for selfish gain," he said with solemn reverence. "Pray each day that your pride will not blind you. Be honourable and courageous; serve others in all you do; love and respect all that God has made. The real war is the one that rages in your heart and mind, Justin. It is a battle that you must fight and win every day of your life."

All the monks knew that Justin had been told about the state of the province. Some knew because Father O'Brien had asked them specifically to pray that Justin would take the news bravely and the rest knew the moment they saw the boy as he arrived for the evening meal. It would have been impossible to describe what it was that was different about his demeanour. He had the same youthful exuberance and childlike innocence but something had changed deep down: he had grown up. The monks were always very kind to Justin but today they took special care. They knew that everything he had to learn before facing the city alone would have to be taught quickly.

Chapter 4

Winter was coming and, though it was not too cold yet, the nights were growing darker. Father O'Brien tried to do most of Justin's physical training before midday, the evenings were spent in the warm glow of candles and fireplaces as they studied the precious books and manuscripts that Justin learned his lessons from.

However, one day, before dusk, Justin was not concentrating well. If the philosophical child had something on his mind he could never focus, and Father O'Brien knew that it was pointless to continue with the studies,

"We will leave it there for today, Justin. You look tired."

Justin blinked quickly and shook himself out of a day dream,

"I'm not tired, Father. I'm just thinking. I'll concentrate now, I promise."

The monk started to clear away the books carefully,

"Let's go for a walk instead. There won't be many more clear evenings like this."

The young scholar and his teacher strolled out into the cool twilight, each with his own private thoughts. After several minutes of silent walking, Justin looked up,

"Father, I've been thinking about when I go to the city. I was wondering, what if the people there don't like me?"

Father O'Brien sighed. He had no intention of deceiving this child,

"Justin, my boy, it will be hard. You might find the people there are very different from those you are used to and, sometimes, you may feel quite lonely. But the truth is, Justin, these people need you: they need you to be a light in a dark place; they need your life to be a healing wind. They may not know it; they may never know it, but this is your chance to give what you have and gain what you want. It has come very soon for you but I believe you are ready."

Justin smiled, he loved it when Father O'Brien spoke like that. It made him feel brave and honourable, like a noble knight. He was so excited about going to the city, but now the time was drawing near he was beginning to discover fears that he did not know he had. He could not imagine life without his friends and family around him and, even with his vibrant imagination, he found it hard to consider a life without green grass, trees, animals and freedom. He smiled to himself as he dreamt that he was describing these wonders of the countryside to the city folk. He painted a picture with his words that left them gasping with amazement and begging him to tell them all he knew.

Father O'Brien looked slightly troubled and several times he started to speak but then stopped. Eventually, he just smiled at Justin and said:

"It is going to be hard, my boy. But I know you will be alright. I will pray for you every day."

Justin thought for a while. He liked the idea of a Heavenly Father who never went away and followed you wherever you went. However, it seemed a bit strange to think that the God that he prayed to help the soldiers on the frontier would also have time to look after a little boy. He supposed it was the same with his real father. Justin knew his father was alive somewhere, but he found it hard to believe that he would ever see him again. A thought struck him which made him feel quite afraid,

"Father, does my real father still love me?" he said in a small voice.

"Of course he does," answered the monk.

"Then why does he not come back?"

Father O'Brien sighed again,

"Justin, I never knew your father very well. But what I do know is that sometimes people have to do things we don't understand exactly because they love us."

"I still don't understand why he can't come back," said Justin quietly, "even for a few days."

Father O'Brien said nothing. He did not understand either but he trusted that Serena did and someday it would become clear. He put a strong hand on the boy's shoulder and they walked in silence for a few minutes. Father O'Brien glanced up. Even in the dim light it was easy to see the dark, heavy clouds that were engulfing the sky and, as he looked, a large drop of rain fell on his face,

"We have walked a bit further than we should have, Justin. I think we will be soaked by the time we get back to the monastery."

Justin was not listening, he was standing stock still, staring into a copse a few feet away, and a cold pair of gleaming eyes was staring back. Father O'Brien took in the situation immediately as he firmly turned the boy around and began walking swiftly back to the monastery with him,

"That is a rogue wolf," he said in a low voice, "he must have been driven out of the pack and he will attack us if he gets a chance. Just stay close, keep walking and don't look at him."

Justin had never been so terrified in his life. Every bone in his body wanted to turn and see if those cold eyes were still following him and every corner of his mind was telling him to run. Father O'Brien was still holding him firmly and Justin resented it. His head was screaming 'why can't we run?' and he found himself doubting that Father O'Brien even knew the danger they were in. The monk sensed the panic rising in the boy and said,

"We just have to make it over this hill. He won't follow us out in the open with the monastery in view."

Justin was sick with fear. He wanted to run. If they ran for the monastery now, surely they would make it over the hill before the wolf caught up with them. He tried to walk faster but Father O'Brien held him back. The rain was now falling heavily and soaking Justin's clothes, making them heavier by the second. At last, he could stand it no longer. He twisted out of the monk's grasp and ran for the brow of the hill as fast as he could.

Justin's mind became a dull blur of wind, rain, and Father O'Brien's voice calling after him frantically. Then, two hard paws hit his back and knocked him to the ground. Completely winded and sick with fear, Justin felt hot breath on his neck and heard a low, savage growl in his ear.

Suddenly, the wolf leapt from the boy's back and Justin turned to see a sight that transfixed him with terror: the wolf was hanging by its teeth from Father O'Brien's left arm. The monk had a long knife in his other hand and with it he stabbed the animal repeatedly until, at last, it went limp and collapsed in a blood-soaked heap.

Justin was in shock and could not move or speak. Father O'Brien dropped the knife and ripped off his bloody habit. He spoke in a voice that was weaker but no less calm than his usual manner,

"We need to get back to the monastery, Justin. Are you hurt?"

Justin could not even shake his head. The rain was now falling heavily and it mingled with the traumatised child's sweat and tears as he stared at his mentor who had blood pouring from an arm which had been bitten to the bone.

"Justin, listen to me. I might not be able to make it back. If I faint, you must get back to the monastery and they will know what to do."

Father O'Brien started to walk and pushed Justin in front of him as they stumbled up the hill. Soon, the monk collapsed and lay very still on the soaking grass. The boy was left standing alone in the driving rain. Justin felt strangely calm in the horror of it all. Deep down he knew that panicking would not help and that he had to decide what to do next by himself. He would be strong now. He had to be strong.

The boy took Father O'Brien's uninjured arm and slung it over his shoulder, carrying the man like a huge sack. Step by agonising step he crept up the hill, after a few metres he stumbled and boy and man collapsed in a heap. Yet, in a few moments they were moving again with Justin chanting 'be strong, be strong' to himself with every laboured breath. He forced his limbs into a rhythm and ignored the pain and exhaustion that threatened to overwhelm him. He was drenched with a freezing liquid which was a mixture of blood and rain mingled with his own sweat. Shaking the hair out of his eyes, he concentrated all his thought into putting one foot in front of the other. At last, he climbed over the brow of the hill.

Suddenly, an icy wind battered his frame and blinded his vision. Justin's fighting spirit rose to his defence and, yelling his defiance to the wind and weather, he battled on towards the dark bulk of the monastery. It was not long, however, before he stumbled once more and this time his exhausted body refused the order to get up again. An undeniable logic told him to rest a while then carry on, but he knew that if he stopped now he might never get up again. Yet he could not make himself move. Countless times he thought he had managed to struggle to his feet, only to find that he was still lying on the ground.

His thoughts became frighteningly clear. In his mind he saw the wolf attacking Father O'Brien and saw himself running for his life. It was all his fault. He had been a coward; he had disobeyed Father O'Brien; he had broken his promise to be strong. His thoughts strayed to his mother. What would she do if they never came back? Would his father return to his family one day and find that his son was not there waiting for him?

If he had a Father in Heaven now seemed a good time to ask Him for help. Justin summoned the last of his strength and cried as loud as he could: 'help!' His voice sounded strange and shrill in his ears and the storm almost drowned it out completely. No answer met his cries and no strength returned to his limbs, nonetheless, Justin was sure he felt something change. Maybe he was just slipping away, but he suddenly felt calm and secure inside. Something seemed to be telling him that he did not have to worry; that he did not have to blame himself; that everything would be alright.

After a few minutes, Justin heard a low voice gently speaking his name in his ear and a light shining in his face. Then a strong pair of arms lifted him and wrapped him in something warm and dry and he was surrounded by urgent voices. Justin murmured 'Father O'Brien?'

"He is fine. Rest now," the voice answered. Justin smiled weakly and said and thought nothing more.

When he regained consciousness he was lying on a feather mattress in his own nightshirt and his clothes were washed and dried at the foot of the bed. Midday light streamed through the window and shone on the golden hair of his mother who was smiling down at him. She took his hand but said nothing. She did not need to: the relief, the pride and the joy in her eyes said it all.

Chapter 5

The weeks leading up to Justin's departure were filled with anticipation and excitement. Father O'Brien made a full recovery, though his arm had to be supported in a sling for several weeks. A huge celebration was organised by the Brothers to praise Justin for his bravery. The storm had raged for almost two days and, had Justin not managed to pull them both up the hill, they might well have perished that night. Justin accepted the praise with great pleasure and approached his journey to the city with a new confidence: he was a light in the darkness, a healing wind, a knight on a noble crusade. In his day dreams, the boys at the cathedral gasped with admiration as he told them the story of how he had escaped from a rogue wolf and saved the great Father O'Brien's life.

Justin wore his sword all the time (though he allowed himself to be convinced to take it off during chapel and choir practise and at night it hung above his bed). He was the envy of every child in the village who, by now, had started to view him as a boy who was verging on the immortal!

The preparations for Justin's move to the city were made: Father O'Brien was to deliver Samson as Lord Athelstan's new war horse and it had been arranged that Justin should be taken to the cathedral choir school at the same time. The choirmaster would hear Justin when he arrived and decide if he was good enough to sing in the cathedral choir.

So it was that Justin stood on the morning of his departure, beaming with excitement, his sack on his back, his sword around his waist and ready to meet his destiny. His mother hugged her son tightly one last time. She did not seem sad or worried, just very proud of her boy and his achievements. There was no hint of a tear in her eye or a sigh in her voice as she said her final goodbye,

"Goodbye my treasure, I will pray for you every day. I love you."

Justin was old enough to guess that his mother wished that he was not going away. He knew that she was letting him go because she loved him, and how he loved her for it. It was a strange feeling to kiss her one last time and turn his back on her. He had done it so many times and yet, this time, it was completely different. He was leaving his family and his home, and it was his decision to do so.

Justin was hauled up onto Samson and they cantered down the road to the city. The days were now short and cold and Justin huddled into his cape as the icy wind battered his body. Father O'Brien was fairly quiet and contemplative and did not speak to Justin much. The two of them knew each other so well now they were able to spend long periods in silence without it seeming awkward, but today it did feel as if certain things were being left unsaid.

Justin's first glance of the city was one he would not soon forget. He was becoming drowsy as they cantered over the brow of the last hillock but was jerked into full reality as thousands of buildings suddenly lay sprawling before them like a grey ocean. Brick houses stretched as far as the eye could see and the cathedral, looking magnificent and terrifying, towered above hundreds of billows of wood smoke. A high stone wall surrounded the city and, further away, Justin spotted the battlemented walls of the keep where Lord Athelstan resided. He saw streets seething with horses and people, looking like swarming ants.

It all seemed bigger, greyer and more intimidating than Justin could ever have imagined from the maps he had studied and he began to experience his first hint of nerves. Samson clattered up to the city gates and Father O'Brien handed a letter to a guard in chain mail who looked at it briefly then handed it back and waved them through. They trotted through the paved streets and Justin stared at everyone. They were so different from the people he was used to: all in a hurry and looking as if they were going somewhere very important. There was a lot of noise and quite a lot of pushing and cursing, and a strong smell of smoke and horse clinging to every street. No-one seemed to notice Justin; if they did, they were not at all interested in him.

Eventually, the paved streets turned to green grass as they trotted under the archway which led them through the perimeter wall of the cathedral close. Justin found himself surrounded by sweet-smelling trees and several ornate buildings, all overshadowed by the imposing cathedral. He craned his neck to gaze in wonder at the colossal building and could not help feeling small and overwhelmed. Father O'Brien lifted Justin from Samson and set him on his feet. The monk knelt down beside the boy and looked him in the eye,

"It will be hard, Justin, but you'll be alright. These people don't know that they need you yet, just don't let them knock it out of you."

"Knock what out of me, Father?"

Father O'Brien smiled and gripped the boy's shoulder,

"You. Don't let them steal the thing that makes you special. When people see someone different from themselves they are afraid and want to prove that they are better, so they try to bring him down. Don't let them."

Justin tried to keep his voice calm,

"But I don't understand, Father. How am I different?"

"Because you are kind, and you know how to trust and... my dear boy, I know you don't understand, but someday you will. Just be the wonderful child that you are and try not to be discouraged. Promise me you will do that."

Justin took a deep breath and said,

"I promise, Father. I am going to be strong."

Father O'Brien smiled again and hugged him tightly with his uninjured arm. Justin felt anything but strong in the vice-like grip, but he hoped that one day he would be.

Justin did not want his friend and mentor to let go, but the longer he delayed the harder it would be. Father O'Brien stood up and placed a hand on the boy's head. He said something quietly in Latin which Justin knew was a blessing. He did feel stronger after it; stronger, warmer and ready to face his destiny.

A tall, thin old man soon emerged from one of the buildings and spoke briefly with the monk. The man enquired about the war and looked at Justin several times, before studying the letter. Justin heard Father O'Brien say 'look after him' in what was almost a warning tone and the man nodded absently. Father O'Brien then approached Justin,

"Justin, this is Master Rickson, Master of Choristers at the cathedral. He will take you to your room."

Justin smiled warmly and bowed. Master Rickson nodded briefly,

"Welcome to the cathedral, Justin."

Father O'Brien then mounted Samson and, with a last smile to Justin, trotted out of the close.

Justin had never felt so alone.

Master Rickson said flatly 'come along then' and Justin followed him into the choir school. His first glimpse of the interior of the building revealed a long corridor with a wooden staircase at one end and a stone archway, leading to what was presumably the kitchen, at the other. Master Rickson led Justin up the long spiral of creaking stairs to a large attic room strewn with mattresses. Three boys were clustered at the far side of the room. Master Rickson addressed them,

"Boys, this is our new probationer from the country. See that he knows the rules and gets settled in."

The boys mumbled an affirmative and Master Rickson departed. Justin stood at the door feeling as awkward as he had ever felt and the boys looked him up and down thoroughly. One of them muttered something to the others and they all stifled a laugh, he then stood up and approached Justin,

"I'm Jonathan Winters, Assistant Head Chorister. Here's what you need to know. Always arrive on time for rehearsal; when you hear the bell you have two minutes to get to the cathedral. One minute late will earn you seven strokes, more than that and it is fourteen. Don't sing wrong notes or sing flat in rehearsal and learn the chants and responses the night before. Never sing at the wrong time in a service or you're for it. Don't even think about getting your surplice dirty – not that you will have one – and don't snore or talk in your sleep, or else... Any questions?"

Justin shook his head. Jonathan pointed towards the door,

"That's your bed over there. Next to Smyth and Chaucer. Smyth is another probationer, Chaucer is an idiot. Matron comes in to check once every night so always pretend to be asleep or you'll get a thrashing. How old are you?"

"Ten."

"And still a probationer? Oh dear. Do you know your gamut?"

"Yes."

"Good. I don't want you losing us spur money. If you have any more questions... ask God!"

Jonathan and the other boys laughed mirthlessly. Justin looked at them, uncertain what the joke was. At that moment, a single loud bell sounded from the cathedral and the boys sprinted down the stairs. Justin pursued and followed them out of the choir school and across the close to the cathedral. They entered through a side door where Master Rickson was standing with a sand timer. Then they slowed to a walk along a narrow corridor where several other boys were processing with solemn dignity. The corridor had small rooms at intervals along it and at the end there was a door that led directly to the quire of the cathedral where the boys would sing.

Justin glanced around as he was swept through the door and towards the choir stalls. He caught his breath: he was surrounded by the most stunning architecture in the largest space he had ever seen. As he gazed down the endless nave, a strange feeling swept through his body, a feeling similar to when he had first heard the monks singing in the monastery. His head felt weightless and his legs felt weak as his eyes traced the magnificent stone arches which stretched elegantly up to meet one another amid the dark, towering roof. He wanted to fall to his knees as he tried to digest the majesty of the building.

Suddenly Justin became aware that he had stopped moving and that the other boys were streaming past him. He hastily joined the line again, though he could not stop himself from staring around in wonder as he did so. The boys smiled condescendingly to themselves: they had expected to have some such naive display from a country boy and he had not disappointed them.

Master Rickson stood in front of the choir stalls and the boys moved swiftly into their places. Justin stood awkwardly to one side and the choirmaster turned to him.

"What is your name, boy?"

"Justin."

"Not your Christian name, your father's name."

In the moment, Justin could not remember what his father's name was. It had never mattered before. Eventually it came to him:

"William."

"It was a simple enough question, Williams. Here," he pointed to a space on his left, "Cantoris side."

Justin took his place and the rehearsal began. The boys sang with strength and confidence, and Justin joined them, though with a subdued voice. Good training meant that Justin sight-read the music easily but during one of the chants in two parts, he sang one note a tone higher than the rest of the choir. Everyone instantly stared at him and Master Rickson stopped them singing and turned to Justin.

"I sang my part, sir," said Justin displaying his music. Master Rickson snatched it and studied it briefly.

"Whoever copied this is as careless as he is lazy. Who was it?"

Silence. Master Rickson handed the part back with a scowl and the rehearsal continued.

Justin became lost in the beauty of the music. Even when Master Rickson continually shouted at them that they were flat and threatened to whip the next person who forgot to sharpen their leading notes; even when the boys beside him started complaining bitterly about the choirmaster and the quality of the chant in low voices; even then, it did not remove the magic.

After the rehearsal, the boys were given a short break before the evensong began and Justin found himself bombarded with questions from the older boys about who he was and where he had come from. But this scene was not as he had always imagined it would be. Instead of the enraptured audience he had envisaged, they did not seem at all interested in hearing his stories or descriptions of his home. The boys could not imagine what he found to fill his time with in the wilderness of the countryside and how he survived the drudgery of small-town life. They nodded to each other, patronisingly, when he told them he had been educated at a monastery. None of them had ever heard of Father O'Brien and did not seem remotely interested that he had once taught King Henry or that Justin had arrived on the war horse which had been bred for the personal use of Lord Athelstan. On the whole, the boys gave the impression that they had nothing to learn from Justin and that he had everything to learn from them, and they seemed so confident and assured that he was tempted to believe them.

It already seemed like an age since Father O'Brien had laid a hand of blessing on Justin's head then disappeared out of the close. The monk's final words seemed like a distant memory now but they still echoed in Justin's ears:

"My dear boy, I know you don't understand, but someday you will. Just be the wonderful child that you are and try not to be discouraged..."

How Justin wished that he did understand now. The cathedral did not seem to need him at all and the other boys certainly did not; everything that he had ever thought precious and sacred was nothing more than a daily routine here. He had nothing to give them.

The boys trooped to the choir school to get robed for the service and the bustling, wordless Matron hastily fitted Justin with a red cassock. It was heavier and richer than the one he was used to wearing and came right down to his ankles. He reached for a white surplice but Jonathan intercepted him,

"Are you having delusions of grandeur already, Williams!" he sneered, "you don't get a surplice until you are a full foundation chorister, surely even you know that."

The lay clerks joined the boys and pulled on their robes as they complained loudly about the choirmaster and the poor pay. White robed servers then entered, talking loudly and, like everyone else, completely ignoring the choirboys. All fell silent as Master Rickson himself arrived and everyone formed an orderly line in the corridor. Justin was paired with Smyth whose probationer status, like Justin, was indicated by his lack of surplice. Justin flashed his partner a quick smile but the little boy turned away awkwardly.

Master Rickson then announced,

"Let us proceed in peace." To which the choir responded,

"In the name of the Lord. Amen."

An ornate cross was then lifted high and the choir followed the crucifer towards the main entrance of the cathedral. Justin felt an indescribable thrill of excitement as they processed solemnly past the cloisters, through the arched entrance way, and into the huge building. As they walked up the long nave, he became aware of the smattering of people on either side him who were standing or kneeling with heads bowed. He knew he must not turn to look at them but, out of the corner of his eye, he noticed that the congregation nearest the quire were better dressed than the others. Sitting in the quire itself were the white robed canons and the most wealthy of the city. Some were kneeling, others had their hands clasped in front of them, but some were sitting with no indication of piety or humility and eyed the choir critically as they took their place in the stalls. One such man drew Justin's eye, he had the look of one whom it would be very unwise to offend. Despite his appearance of being well advanced in years, he was extremely tall and muscular and a fierce pair of eyes glowered from his gaunt face. He sat in a full suit of armour which was engraved with a coat of arms.

The man sat through the service seemingly unmoved. He frequently stared directly at Justin and the other boys as if he was examining them thoroughly. Justin tried to ignore it but the man had such a powerful presence he found it impossible to do so. The service continued and the boys sang beautifully, filling the cavernous cathedral with celestial music. When the last echoes had faded from the rafters, they processed out in silence.

The moment the boys were out of the building they began chattering excitedly:

"Did you see who was sitting in the quire?"

"Earl Guy hardly ever comes to the cathedral! Even on feast days."

"He's the richest man in the province. We must try to get some spur money."

"He'll never give us spur money."

"We have to try, send the probationers."

Jonathan approached Justin and Smyth,

"You two, run and ask Earl Guy for spur money."

"What is spur money?" asked Justin innocently.
Jonathan turned to the chorister next to him and rolled his eyes,

"He doesn't know what spur money is!" he turned to Justin again,

"If a knight comes to the cathedral in a full suit of armour and wearing spurs the choristers are allowed to ask him for spur money. You do know what a suit of armour is, don't you?"

Justin ignored the remark and ran into the cathedral with Smyth. They ducked under the crowds that were streaming down the nave and met the earl as he left the quire, surrounded by his entourage of half a dozen men in chain mail. The two boys rushed up to the Earl energetically. He sneered on seeing them, but put on a forced smile as Justin bowed and said,

"Spur money please, your honour?"

Earl Guy turned to Smyth,

"Do you know your gamut, boy?"

Smyth nodded eagerly and sang the complicated scale loud and clear. People passing nearby, stopped to watch the encounter. The earl took a handful of gold coins from one of his servants and held them out to Smyth. The little boy gasped in excitement and put out a hand to take them. Suddenly, Earl Guy withdrew his hand and struck Smyth across the face. The boy staggered and stumbled to the ground amid roaring laughter from Earl Guy and his company.

Justin was seized with rage and, before he knew it, he was shouting up at Earl Guy,

"What did you do that for!"

The stunned silence that followed told Justin that his question had been inappropriate, and one look at the earl's face left him in no doubt what his next move should be. He grabbed Smyth by the arm and sprinted out of the cathedral as fast as his ankle-length cassock would allow. Smyth was still reeling from the blow and, as soon as they were safely back in the choir school, he collapsed on the ground. The other boys crowded round,

"Did you get any money? What's wrong with Smyth?"

"We got a slap in the face and nothing else," replied Justin pushing them away. The boys laughed mirthlessly and left them alone. Justin felt the anger rising up in him again but he forced it down and, instead, knelt down next to Smyth. He was not badly hurt but was quite shocked by the unwarranted attack, Justin knew that he should distract him and make him think about something else so he said,

"What is your real name?"

Smyth stared at him blankly. Justin tried again,

"You know, your Christian name. The name your parents gave you?"

"Arthur," answered the boy in his delicate young voice.

"That's much nicer than Smyth," said Justin smiling. "I'll call you Arthur if you don't mind."

Arthur said nothing and turned away. He did not want Justin to see the emotion which hearing his first name provoked, no-one had called him that since he left his doting mother and proud father four months ago. He desperately wanted to be one of the big boys who were so clever and confident. They did not seem to like Justin much and so Arthur had avoided him. But this strange boy from the country was kind to him: perhaps the others were wrong...

"I would rather you called me Justin than Williams," said Justin gently, "nobody calls me Williams at home."

Arthur nodded and smiled very slightly. Suddenly, he wanted to tell Justin all about his home and how much he missed it, but words would not come. He started to feel very homesick. He had been numb until now: unable to feel anything as he was swept along in the relentless routine. But Justin had aroused in him emotions that he had not dared to feel before. Until today, happiness had been a long forgotten dream, but Justin's simple compassion had re-kindled the innocent trust of his early childhood. Arthur looked up with trust in his young eyes and Justin smiled at him in his warm honest way.

At that moment, one of the older boys walked in. Justin had noticed that this boy never seemed to join in with the others' jokes and jibes, yet they seemed to give him a grudging respect. He was almost a head taller than every other choirboy and must have been 14 or 15. He looked at the two probationers for a moment then asked, "Is everything alright?" in a matter-of-fact manner. Justin looked up,

"Yes, Arthur got hit by the earl for asking for spur money but he is alright now."

"Earl Guy! Who told you to ask the earl for spur money?"

"Winters."

The boy gave a sigh of exasperation,

"Never mind. Come and get something to eat, it will be time for bed soon."

They followed him to the large stone kitchen where the other boys were sitting at a long wooden table. The big bustling matron was serving them broth from a pot and indicated two free seats with her ladle. The room was pleasantly warm and there was a strangely quiet and friendly tone to the conversations of the young choristers. Justin and Arthur were mostly ignored but nobody overlooked them when the food was distributed. Something about the serene atmosphere suggested to Justin that perhaps, someday, he might look on this place like a home. When the boys had eaten, they began to drift to the attic dormitory. Justin had no idea what the procedure was and followed Arthur as closely as possible as they got ready for bed. The younger boy did not offer any encouragement to Justin but neither did he resent his shadowing of him. He remembered all too well his first night in the choir school: how he was tolerated rather than welcomed and referred to only as 'the probationer' by everyone.

Buckets of water heated on the kitchen fire were brought up to the dormitory so the boys could wash themselves. This they did with careless efficiency by pulling off their tunics and splashing their faces and necks with water. The beds had wide, straw-filled mattresses and a space underneath to store belongings. The room smelled old and damp but, thanks to the lack of windows, it was not as cold as the harsh winter might have made it. An oil lamp on a stool in the middle of the room gave the only illumination, but it was enough for Justin to see the faces of the other boys as they pulled on their nightshirts and clambered onto their mattresses. Lots of them were watching him as he sat on his bed which was near the door. He did not appreciate the attention and started to feel that it was going to be very difficult to sleep in these strange surroundings, even though he was exhausted.

He felt under the bed until he found his own nightshirt and laid it carefully on the corner of his mattress. Chaucer, the tall boy who had spoken to them earlier, was on his left and Arthur was on his right. When everyone else had washed, Justin took off his tunic and, shivering, splashed his face with the now lukewarm water.

Jonathan Winters crept up behind him. Suddenly, he pushed Justin's head under the water and held it there. Justin burst to the surface, coughing and gasping for breath. The first thing he heard as the water drained from his ears was the ringing laughter of almost every boy in the room. Jonathan stood grinning with his arms folded,

"Sorry about that Williams. You have now been baptised into the world of the dormitory!"

"Thanks," spluttered Justin, not without irony. He started to move towards his bed but was intercepted by Jonathan,

"Where are you going? You were last; it's your job to put the water buckets back in the kitchen. Just leave them in the doorway and then you can go to bed."

It took Justin the best part of fifteen minutes to move all the water. He dragged the buckets down the spiral staircase and along the corridor taking utmost care not to spill a drop. By the time he came up the stairs for the final time everyone had lost interest in him. They were lying across their mattresses talking to each other and giggling quite a lot. Justin tried to fight the feeling that they were all laughing at him but he was swiftly becoming paranoid. Chaucer and Arthur did not tease him like the other boys but neither did they stand up for him, he was starting to feel very much alone as he put on his nightshirt and prepared for bed.

Justin had never had any qualms about standing up for himself, but everything was so different here. It felt as if had been transported to another world where he did not belong, a world so strange that he did not know how to react to it.

As he stared around at the chattering groups of boys he knew that his previous impression had been wrong: he would never be one of them, and he did not want to be. Questions gyrated in his mind. Why should he struggle to be accepted in a place that did not want him when he had a home that would always welcome him with open arms? Where did he really belong? He had spent his young life dreaming about being somewhere like this, but now he just wanted to be back home...

In spite of these insecurities, Justin did not seek any permission nor hesitate for a moment before his next move: he knelt down by his bed, clasped his hands and started to say his prayers. Gradually whispers in the room turned to giggles, and giggles turned to raucous laughter. Jonathan shouted across the room,

"I knew you hadn't made many friends yet, Williams, but I didn't realise you were that desperate!"

Justin clenched his teeth in embarrassment and rage but said nothing other than a whispered prayer for self-control. Jonathan was not finished, however. He came to the middle of the room and jeered sarcastically,

"I wish I was as holy as you! Is that something you learned at your monastery?"

That was the last straw. Mocking him was one thing, mocking his monastery was quite another. Justin squared up to his tormentor,

"Yes and here's something else I learned at my monastery ..."

With a smooth, swift movement, he grabbed Jonathan's arm and threw him to the ground. For a few seconds, a shocked silence filled the room. Then, Jonathan attacked with violent fury. Justin was unprepared for the sudden ferocity and would have taken quite a beating if, at that moment, Chaucer had not pulled them apart,

"That's enough, Winters," he shouted, pushing them to either side of the room.

"He attacked me! Let me at him!" yelled Jonathan, still livid.

"I'm still head chorister and I say he's had enough for one night. You've been teasing him all day and you got what you deserved."

Jonathan went to bed scowling and muttering threats. Eventually, everyone started to settle down. Justin climbed into his bed and lay on his stomach. He buried his face in the pillow and felt his heart thumping against the mattress, his exhausted mind was too tired to even begin processing what had just happened or imagine what tomorrow might bring. Within in a few minutes he had drifted into a deep, dreamless sleep.

Chapter 6

Justin awoke to the sound of a crash and a yell from the kitchen downstairs. Morning light streamed from the doorway and revealed the boys in various stages of tumbling out of bed and getting dressed. Jonathan sat on the side of his bed, fully dressed and grinning,

"Morning Williams. I think matron has found your buckets. Better go and bring them up so we can wash ourselves before breakfast."

"But you told me I had to take them down last night," protested Justin.

"I lied."

Suddenly, Matron entered in a foul temper, growling,

"Who put the wash buckets in the kitchen doorway? Own up or I'll thrash the lot of you."

A few of the boys pointed to Justin who desperately pointed to Jonathan,

"He told me to. I didn't know. I thought ..."

"Don't make excuses, boy. Take them all back up double quick and I'll maybe leave your whipping until after breakfast. And you're not even dressed yet — you're just asking for it now."

Justin looked around the room hopelessly for some support. Jonathan was the only one who seemed to find the situation amusing; the other boys were all staring blankly at the ground. Chaucer spoke up,

"Matron, the buckets were not William's fault. He only arrived yesterday and he is still learning."

Matron scrutinised Justin,

"Oh you're the new one. Hurry up and get dressed, you'll be late for breakfast."

Matron brought up the buckets herself and even filled them with fresh water. She carried four at a time as if they were filled with feathers. Seeing Justin's despondent expression, she knelt beside him and spoke with an attempt at a gentle tone,

"I can see that you were trying to help, Williams. The boys try to wind me up a lot you see. Are you enjoying the cathedral?"

Justin nodded meekly and Matron continued,

"I don't understand it all really, but I must say you boys make a lovely sound when you all sing together. Now go and get washed and get your clothes on."

The water was freezing cold and woke Justin up enough for the memories of last night to come flooding back. He kept a wary eye on Jonathan at all times.

Breakfast was a clinical affair and no-one spoke much, not that that there was much to speak about. When all the boys were fed they trooped over to the cathedral for Matins. Master Rickson greeted them formally before handing out the appropriate chants and starting the vocal warm-up. Justin was still tired and was not concentrating well. There was no time to wake up properly before the service and he had a horrible feeling that he might not be able to sing accurately.

The boys were joined by the men and they all robed and took their places in the choir stalls. During the reading, Justin hastily looked over the chants but the notes were dancing before his eyes and the moment he had memorised one he forgot another. He made his first mistake during the responses and Master Rickson instantly glared at him. From then on it got worse as nerves took their toll on his concentration. He sang several wrong notes, and, on one occasion, he was focusing on his music so hard that he forgot to watch the choirmaster and he came in a beat early. Justin left the service feeling completely drained, and yet only too sure that he would soon be disciplined.

Master Rickson approached him as he was removing his cassock. Justin tried to avoid eye contact, but the choirmaster swung the boy round causing his cassock to fall to the ground,

"Did you learn those chants, Williams?"

"No sir," answered Justin timidly.

"What were you doing last night?"

Justin started to tremble,

"Nothing, sir."

"Then why did you not learn the chants?"

"I forgot, sir."

Master Rickson leaned over the boy imposingly,

"Well, do not forget again. I understand that you have only been here a short while, but usually a boy would be whipped for singing at the low standard you gave me this morning. Only the very highest quality is acceptable in this cathedral. Do you understand?"

Justin lowered his eyes,

"Yes sir, I am sorry sir," he said in a small voice.

Master Rickson walked briskly out of the room. Jonathan snorted,

"Yes sir, no sir, sorry sir, please don't whip me sir," he mocked in a high pitched voice. The boys next to him obediently joined in a chorus of half-hearted laughter.

Justin pretended not to hear and Jonathan continued his impersonation by kneeling on the floor and pretending to pray,

"Dear Lord, please don't let me be whipped and please don't let anyone notice that I am the worst singer in the cathedral."

He then stood up, pushed Justin,

"Come on then Williams," he snarled, "finish what you started last night."

Justin was almost too exhausted to stand, far less fight, and he tried to walk out of the room. Jonathan pushed him again and the rest of the excited boys started to form a circle around them. Justin tried to struggle out of the ring,

"I don't want to fight. Leave me alone."

Jonathan kicked him in the leg and forced him to the ground,

"You were keen enough to start it last night, Williams. Gives it but can't take it — that's you."

Justin shouted up at his tormentor,

"You deserved what you got last night, Chaucer even said so."

This was all the provocation Jonathan needed, he leapt on Justin and pounded him relentlessly. Justin feebly tried to defend himself, but his opponent had the upper hand and was much bigger and stronger than him. Jonathan forced Justin's arms above his head and hit him in the face repeatedly.

A moment later, Chaucer dashed in and hauled Jonathan off,

"What are you two playing at?" he shouted. "Winters, didn't I tell you to stop tormenting Williams? He's just a probationer."

Jonathan mumbled something inaudible and turned away. Chaucer swung him round again,

"What's that, Winters? If you have something to say, then say it."

Jonathan stamped his foot in frustration,

"You didn't say anything when Williams threw me and almost broke my neck just because he couldn't take a joke. He's younger so he gets away with anything."

"That's not what I'm talking about," shouted Chaucer. "You are supposed to be Assistant Head Chorister. No matter what you think of him, this is no way for a cathedral chorister to behave. And that goes for all of you. The next person I catch bullying or fighting will answer to me."

Chaucer then knelt down next to Justin, who had a bleeding nose and a bruised right eye,

"You alright, Williams?" he asked without emotion.

Justin was angry and very shocked but not seriously injured. He held a hand to his bleeding nose,

"I didn't do anything that time," he gasped between breaths, "why does Winters hate me so much?"

"You injured his pride and he wants revenge. He will leave you alone now. Smyth, run to the kitchen and fetch a wet rag for Williams before he starts bleeding all over the cassocks."

Arthur ran out, glad to be released from the tense atmosphere and keen to help Justin. Matron entered and the boys crowding around Justin instantly dispersed,

"What have you boys been doing now?" She looked down at Justin, who was now sitting with his back against the wall,

"Don't tell me you've been fighting already, Williams!"

"It's under control, Matron," said Chaucer, calmly standing up. "Williams might need an hour or two to himself in the dormitory."

Arthur dashed in with a wet cloth and handed it to Justin. The boys came towards him again and Matron pushed them away,

"Give him some space boys. Smyth, go up with him and see that he lies down."

Justin staggered upstairs holding the rag to his nose. Arthur hung up Justin's cassock for him then followed on quietly as the other boys dispersed.

Justin dragged himself to the dormitory then collapsed onto his bed. Arthur entered and stood awkwardly for a few moments, and then he approached slowly,

"Are you badly hurt, Williams... I mean, Justin?"

Justin rolled over to look gratefully at Arthur,

"I'll be alright. I just wish Winters would leave me alone though." He added defiantly, "I could beat him if I wanted, you know."

Arthur said nothing, but stared in admiration of this country boy's wild spirit. Justin heaved himself into a sitting position,

"How did he get to be assistant head chorister anyway? He's meant to be looking after the younger boys like Chaucer does, not trying to ..."

Justin clasped the bloody rag to his face as his nose started to flow again. Arthur glanced nervously at the door, afraid that someone might be listening,

"Winters can be nice when he wants to," said Arthur, "and he's the best singer next to Chaucer. It's just tradition to annoy the new boys, especially on the first night. I'm sure it happened to Winters when he was a probationer."

"Then he must know how horrible it is," frowned Justin. "Perhaps he'll stop now. At least, Chaucer stands up for me."

Arthur looked down at his feet and said hesitantly,

"Justin, I just want you to know that... if it would do any good, I would... but it wouldn't you see..." suddenly he blurted out, "I'm sorry I don't stand up for you, Justin."

"I didn't mean that Arthur," said Justin quickly, surprised at the sudden outburst, "I should never have thrown Winters in the first place. He only wants revenge, like Chaucer said. It's my own fault, really."

Arthur clasped Justin's stained hand,

"No Justin, I should have said something. I know you would have done the same for me. But I... I'm a coward."

"You're not a coward, Arthur," said Justin sincerely. "You are very strong to have survived on your own all this time. I don't know if I would have lasted as long in this place."

"But I didn't survive it," cried Arthur, unable to stem the flow of his emotions, "two weeks after I arrived I couldn't bear it any longer and I sent a letter to my father asking him to take me home again. He replied and said that if I didn't become a man now, I never would and that I had to stay. I cried all that night and the next one and I had to stop myself from thinking about home every day or I would start crying again. I'm not strong at all."

"There is nothing wrong with letting your feelings out before they get the better of you," said Justin kindly. "That way you can deal with them and..."

He stopped, suddenly realising that he had quoted Father O'Brien. Justin felt a little thrill of excitement: this was it! This was what Father O'Brien had said about being a light a dark place and a healing wind. This was his chance to give what he had: he could help Arthur.

Arthur looked up gratefully and said delicately,

"Justin, could we be friends?"

Justin smiled warmly,

"Yes, Arthur, let's be friends."

Justin had never seen Arthur smile. Suddenly a timid, frightened child became a bright, carefree boy who was filled with energy. He jumped up gleefully,

"I'm so glad you came to the cathedral, Justin. I feel like I've been in a dark room all this time and now someone has just thrown back the shutters and let the sunshine in!"

They both laughed with youthful exuberance and the two boys then sat talking for almost an hour. They exchanged stories of their homes and families and listened to each other with genuine interest. When the bell rang for the afternoon meal they washed then ran happily down the stairs together.

Arthur observed that everything seemed better with a friend to share it with: the winter sun was warmer, the plain food tasted sweeter, and, best of all, the harsh judgement of others seemed almost irrelevant. Jonathan was clearly tempted to direct some tasteless comment towards the two young friends but he said nothing. Justin's eye was now visibly and painfully swollen and there was a general feeling among the choristers that Jonathan had gone somewhat too far on this occasion.

Justin noticed that Chaucer had not been at the meal and he did not see him for the rest of the day. When bedtime came he was still nowhere to be seen and Justin was shocked to see that Chaucer's belongings were no longer under his bed. Justin turned urgently to a boy who was laying out his nightshirt,

"Where is Chaucer? All his things are gone."

"Haven't you heard?" answered the boy carelessly, "his voice has broken and he left today. It was going to happen soon or later. He's got a job as a server in the cathedral."

"But... but he didn't even say goodbye..."

"He did. You weren't there."

The boy walked away and Justin stared helplessly after him.

So that was that. Chaucer was gone and Jonathan would soon be head chorister.

Justin washed, pulled on his nightshirt, then said his prayers and climbed into bed. He tried to imagine that he was at the top of a high tower, safe and secure; or floating in a sturdy boat far out at sea. It was becoming harder every day to lose himself in imaginary worlds and it took all his concentration to forget his troubles and focus on his day dream. Eventually, he succeeded and soon he had drifted into a blissful sleep.

Justin was woken in the middle of the night by the sound of the wind wailing round his tower; or was it the sea birds calling above his boat? He was jerked into reality as he suddenly remembered where he was and perceived that the sound he was hearing came from the bed next to his.

Justin rubbed his bleary eyes and peered around the dark room. He could hear the deep, slow breathing of the sleeping boys in the room but, beside him, Arthur was sobbing pitifully into his pillow.

"What's the matter Arthur?" whispered Justin gently.

Arthur was neither fully awake nor fully asleep. He clutched Justin's hand and sobbed,

"I want to go home. Why can't I go home?"

Justin tried to comfort the weeping child,

"You can go home soon. You just need to hang on for a few weeks. You don't need to be sad."

"I want to go home now," sobbed Arthur. "I don't want to stay here anymore."

Justin did not know what to say, so he held the little boy's hand and stroked his hair, as his mother always did for him when he woke up from a nightmare. Justin imitated her soothing tone,

"But we're not here, Arthur. We're at the top a high tower, the strongest tower in the world. And it's warm and safe and there's stacks of good food below us, and it's our tower and we can do whatever we like..."

Eventually, Arthur's cries faded and he drifted into a heavy slumber. Justin noticed a crumpled piece of paper on the pillow next to Arthur's open hand. He carefully removed it and squinted to read; it was the letter from Arthur's father. It said a good deal about how proud he was of his dear son and how they all missed him, but it ended with the firm statement: 'if you cannot learn to be a man now, you will never be a man'. Justin felt strange as he read those words. He could not remember ever having been forced to grow up, he realised that Arthur had probably been sent to the choir school against his will and given no choice in the matter. Now he understood: Arthur wanted to please his parents; he wanted to be a man, but he did not believe that he was strong enough to do it.

Justin lay down again and thought of his home. He thought of how keen he had been to leave and how his friends would be assuming that he was having a wonderful time right now. How he missed it... but he had to stay. He had promised that he would be strong and, besides, he had to stay for Arthur. It was the first time in Justin's life that he had ever felt really needed by someone else and it gave him a reason to carry on.

In the morning, as the boys started to stir one by one, it seemed that Arthur had no recollection of his nightly sorrow. He started getting washed and dressed happily enough until Justin returned the letter to him. At first, Arthur accepted it with curiosity, but then, as the memories came flooding back, he dropped his eyes to hide his shame and his cheeks flushed red with embarrassment,

"Some man I am," he muttered. "I hate myself."

"You mustn't say that, Arthur."

"Why not?"

Justin was not sure why not. He knew that it was wrong but he could not explain why.

After breakfast, the boys robed for Matins. Today, Jonathan was to be promoted to head chorister and one of the older boys would be made the assistant. Everything seemed very strange without Chaucer. Many of the boys had resented his authority, but they had all respected him. Chaucer had been a chorister for years and was one of the most musically gifted boys the cathedral had ever had. However, the choirboys were used to comings and goings and their silent stoicism was essential if they were to prove to their peers that they were experienced choristers.

Justin, however, was not used to comings and goings and had no interest in proving himself to anyone. Chaucer was the only person who had stood up for him, even if he was only doing so out of a sense of responsibility, and Justin felt utterly vulnerable now that he was gone.

During the service the priest called Jonathan out to the altar and laid a hand on his head,

"Do you swear to serve God with all your body, mind and soul?"

"I do."

"Do you swear to fulfil your duties in the instruction and care of the trebles, within both the cathedral and the choir school?"

"I do."

"Do you swear to fulfil such duties which are required of you in good faith and to the glory of Almighty God?"

"I do."

"I now install you head chorister of this cathedral church. In nomine Patris, Filii et Spiritus Sancti. Amen."

Jonathan bowed and crossed himself as he received his red ribbon, then returned to his seat with all due reverence. Justin was becoming accustomed to the way that everyone was expected to display sincerity without feeling any, but he did not understand this behaviour. His innocent heart was still too trusting to believe that someone could make an oath that they had no intention of keeping, or pray to a God that they did not believe in. He doubted that he would ever get used to it. And he did not want to: he hated it.

Chapter 7

In the weeks that followed, Jonathan did very little to torment Justin though he clearly still harboured an acute dislike for him. Either Jonathan Winters was taking his duties as head chorister very seriously or he felt that simply ignoring his enemy was punishment enough. However, one night as everyone was getting changed for bed; Jonathan came up to Justin and pointed to a red mark on his shoulder,

"What is that, Williams?"

"Nothing, it's just a birthmark," said Justin turning away.

Jonathan looked genuinely concerned as he said,

"That's not just a birthmark, Williams. My older brother had one exactly like it."

Justin was not sure whether or not to believe this story, but either way he was unable to resist his own curiosity. He reluctantly turned back to Jonathan,

"What is it?"

Jonathan looked Justin in the eye,

"It's a rare disease, you... I'm sorry, if it is the same as my brother, you are not going to live past twenty, Justin."

Justin looked up on hearing his first name. There was a quiver of emotion in Jonathan's voice. He seemed so sincere it was hard not to believe him but, on the other hand, this was just the sort of trick that he would play.

Justin went to bed lost in thought. A strange, sick feeling gripped him, as when Father O'Brien had told him the state of the province: a horrible truth that he wished was a lie. How could he know? Even if someone else told him that Jonathan was lying, how could he ever be sure? Jonathan had said that his brother had died with that same mark. Surely even Jonathan would not lie about something like that? These thoughts gyrated around his mind until, exhausted, he fell asleep.

The next day, as Justin was sitting with Arthur on the steps of the cathedral, a thin, well-groomed old man approached them. He was dressed in a rich coat and had an air of elegance in his manner,

"Which of you young gentleman is Justin Williams?"

Justin stood up. The old man examined him for moment then smiled,

"Ah yes, you fit the description Father O'Brien gave me."

"Do you know Father O'Brien?" asked Justin eagerly.

The man was somewhat taken aback by Justin's bold reply but he recovered his composure and said,

"Yes, I know him well. He spoke highly of you. Now you must come with me and we must find you something to wear which is suitable for a page of Lord Athelstan. You are not fit to be seen as you are."

"Am I to meet Lord Athelstan today?" asked Justin with excitement.

The man glared at him strictly, but had to clear his throat to hide the hint of an amused smile hovering on his lips,

"His Lordship will require a little more decorum on your part, young man. You will meet him when he calls you. I reminded his Lordship that he had asked for you and, at the time, he seemed keen to have you entertain him. We shall see."

"Can Arthur come, sir?"

"Certainly not. This is not some sort of children's outing. Serving his Lordship requires nothing less than the utmost respect and dignity. Do you understand?"

Justin nodded eagerly and the man took his hand and led him out of the close. They walked briskly along the crowded streets, away from the shadow of the cathedral and towards the towering form of the keep. Justin stared curiously at every citizen who bustled past, and turned his head at every shout or sudden noise. The old man, however, held the boy's hand firmly and ignored every distraction until they arrived at the steps of the great stone keep. Every corner of the imposing building was built for strength but, even so, additional arrow towers supporting the solid, grey walls had recently been built.

Justin gasped as, only a few feet away from him, a dozen riders in chain mail clattered up to the keep and dismounted, suddenly turning the quiet courtyard into a deafening flurry of horses hooves and shouted orders. The old man pulled Justin out of the way as six stableboys dashed out and each grabbed two horses, leading them to the vast stables on the other side of the wall. The riders then removed their helmets and entered the keep.

"That is the patrol back from the eastern border," said the old man. "If it is bad news I doubt that his Lordship will see you today. But we must be ready just in case."

He then led Justin up the steep steps and into the keep. The guards at the door nodded respectfully to the man but ignored Justin completely.

Beyond the door was a great stone hall with a huge banner hanging from the high roof and a banqueting table upturned against the far wall. Many small, studded doors were located around the hall and Justin was guided towards one of these on the left.

Through the door was a room strewn with various garments and materials. A loom stood against the far wall and scented the room with the warm, woolly smell that was so familiar to Justin. A motherly woman in a rich gown was sewing on a stool near the doorway. She smiled on seeing them enter and rose like vapour from her seat,

"Ah, this must be little Justin," she said in a gentle, pleasant voice.

Justin was not too keen on being called 'little', but he was relieved to be greeted with such warmth, so he smiled his sincere smile and nodded cheerfully. The lady gracefully stooped and kissed Justin on the forehead then said cordially,

"My name is Lady Winters. I am a friend of Lord Athelstan and I also oversee the clothing in the castle for him. You will know my Jonathan of course?"

Justin jumped. How could this kind lady be Jonathan's mother? He swiftly hid his shock and answered,

"Yes, Jonathan is head chorister at the cathedral."

"I have seen you singing at the services, you are very good. Now, has Sir James shown you around the castle yet?"

Sir James spoke for Justin,

"It would be best if we got the boy cleaned up first, Lady Winters. His lordship has a lot on his mind, after all, and he might require the boy to wait on him soon."

"Yes, of course," said Lady Winters surveying Justin. "Now, where to begin...? He'll need a good hot bath and we'll have to try to get some of the grime out of that lovely head of hair. Sir James, could you please ask the servants to bring a bath and to heat some water while I start looking out an outfit for our new page to wear?"

Sir James bowed to the lady, smiled at the boy and left the room. Lady Winters finished her sewing quickly then put it down and turned to Justin,

"Now then, where to begin?" she said looking him up and down. "Where to begin... what do you usually wear to special occasions, my dear?"

Justin was slightly nervous that his complete lack of knowledge about finery and fashion was going to get him into trouble. He glanced hesitantly at all the rich clothes in the room,

"I usually just wear my tunic with a clean shirt and hose," answered Justin. Then, deciding that he should be honest, he added, "Actually, I don't have anything else."

He searched for some inspiration, anxious to please Lady Winters,

"My mother used to clean my hair every week and I would wash every morning, or at least I would swim in the lake every morning."

At that moment two servants entered, carrying a tin bath. Lady Winters directed them to put it in a clear space on the floor and, presently, more servants arrived with bowls of steaming water. Justin looked on with interest as, bowl by bowl, the bath began to fill up with water and the room began to fill with a warm steam.

"Is that all for me?" asked Justin, gazing at this fascinating luxury.

"Of course, my dear," said Lady Winters. She poured some perfume into the water from a little glass bottle, "we need you to look your best for Lord Athelstan, and besides, the steam is good for my cloth!"

Justin had never had a bath before. He had never even seen one. He peered through the swirling steam,

"What do I do? Should I stand in the water or is it like a big wash bucket?"

Lady Winters laughed merrily,

"No dear, think of it as a small lake, all for you!"

When the bath was full, Justin pulled off his clothes and climbed into the water. It was hot and clean and he sighed with delight as he felt the warmth of the water on his skin. Lady Winters rolled up her sleeves and poured water over his head using a vase. She scrubbed his hair with her hands,

"Are you trying to grow potatoes in here or did you just want to change the colour of your hair!"

Justin looked up, thinking that he was being reprimanded. Lady Winters laughed,

"Don't worry, dear. I know what boys are like. I've had four."

A thought suddenly struck Justin and asked,

"Where are they now?"

"The oldest two are fighting on the border, Jonathan is the youngest and Peter... well our Peter is in heaven."

"Did he..." Justin controlled his quavering voice. "Did he have a mark like this?" He showed Lady Winters the mark on his shoulder and she examined it curiously,

"Well, yes, he had something like it, but that is not why he died, dear. That is just a harmless birthmark. Peter died of a fever."

"But Jonathan... Jonathan told me..."

"Ah, I see."

Lady Winter's sighed sadly and continued to wash Justin's hair but now with gentle hands,

"You see Justin, Jonathan and Peter were as close as brothers can be but, when they were both little, there was one occasion when they had a bit of a fight. Jonathan was very annoyed at his brother and tried to scare him by pretending that the birthmark on his shoulder was a disease that would kill him. It was not true, of course, and they were best of friends again soon afterwards. But Jonathan did not forget what he said and he still genuinely believes that Peter became ill because of the birthmark. He misses Peter very badly and he feels guilty I think. Jonathan is still a little boy really, and it will take him a while to get over his grief."

Justin paused as he took all this in. It seemed ludicrous to hear Jonathan described as a vulnerable 'little boy', but to a mother it was probably true. Justin could not help feeling an overwhelming sense of pity for his tormentor. He wondered for a fleeting moment if all Jonathan's bravado was in fact nothing more than a frightened child lashing out at the world. Perhaps, deep down, even strong men were 'little boys'...

Justin looked up eagerly,

"Are you sure I'm not going to die?"

Lady Winters pinched Justin's cheek, smiling sincerely,

"Oh, my dear, do not tell me that you have been worrying about a little birthmark. You are a fine, healthy boy; you have nothing to be afraid of."

Justin felt as if a huge, heavy chain had fallen off him. He was not going to die after all! He had already forgiven Jonathan for the lie but now he wondered if it had been more than a lie: perhaps it had been a cry for help.

Lady Winters dried Justin with a warm towel and dressed him in a suit made of purple velvet with a red cape. He wished he had his sword to complete the outfit, but did not suppose he would be allowed to wear it in the presence of Lord Athelstan. Lady Winters stepped back to survey her handiwork,

"My word, what a fine young gentleman! You have beautiful golden hair when it is clean, my dear. You look truly angelic!"

Justin smiled at the praise. He did not mind being called angelic. As far as he could make out, angels spent most of their time wielding fiery swords, not floating around with halos. It would not be such a bad thing to be one of them!

Justin started thinking that it was strange he should be chosen above other boys to do something he had never done before. He looked curiously up at Lady Winters,

"Why did Lord Athelstan want me and not a different boy? I don't think I will be a very good page really."

Lady Winters made the finishing touches to Justin's collar,

"Oh, his lordship insisted on having a country boy. He has lots of city boys to wait on him and he tells me that he finds them..." she put on a mock lordly tone, "very arrogant and mostly irritating! Of course, it was not easy to find a young boy from the country who had the necessary skills, but then Father O'Brien told us about you and it seemed that you were a godsend."

Justin stared vacantly at the roof,

"Is Lord Athelstan a nice man?"

"He is a very wise man for his years; the most honourable lord the province has had for many decades. He never lies or cheats and he is fiercely moral and always sees that his subjects receive justice."

Justin returned his gaze to the woman before him. He thought of the city men that he had encountered so far. He found it hard to imagine the lord being very different from these,

"He won't hurt me or shout at me, will he?" he asked beseechingly.

Lady Winters lowered her eyes for a moment then said gently,

"I should not think anyone would want to hurt you, my dear. But you must understand that his lordship has a lot on his mind. He may be a bit short with you, but it is not because of anything you have said or done wrong. Just be yourself and you will be a great help to him."

At that moment, Sir James entered looking gloomy,

"The border patrol did not bring good news. I doubt that Lord Athelstan will want to see the boy today."

Lady Winter's presented Justin to Sir James,

"But, look Sir James, he is all ready. Perhaps the boy should see his lordship regardless of what he says. It will do his lordship so much good."

"No, Lady Winters that would not be wise."

There was a moment of silence, in which the two exchanged anxious glances. Lady Winters gave in with a sigh,

"Well, I suppose that is the end of the matter. Justin, take these clothes off carefully and try to keep your hair clean until tomorrow."

"Will Lord Athelstan see me tomorrow?" asked Justin, trying to hide his disappointment as he fumbled with the buttons.

"I hope so, my dear. I really do think that you might help him. He has such a lot on his mind... such a lot..."

Justin's old clothes felt rough and dirty after the finery he had been wearing. Sir James escorted him back to the cathedral close and told him to be ready at noon tomorrow. He then ceremonially kissed Justin on the forehead and took his leave.

A faint sound of singing drifted from inside the cathedral and Justin's heart sank: he was late for rehearsal. He dashed into the cathedral and took his place as they were finishing the chant. Master Rickson glared at him,

"If you are late again, Williams, you will be whipped. Understand?"

Justin could see that now was not the time to offer excuses so he simply nodded and prepared the next chant. He noticed that Arthur, who stood opposite him, looked very pale and hoped that nothing had happened to him while he was away. After the rehearsal Arthur stumbled out and Justin knew that he ought to check on him, but he had to speak to Master Rickson and let him know that he was required by Lord Athelstan tomorrow. Master Rickson was speaking to Jonathan about one of the chants and Justin waited patiently until they had finished. When Jonathan had gone Justin looked up at the choirmaster,

"Excuse me, sir..."

"Enough, Williams, just make sure it doesn't happen again."

"Please, sir, it's not that... I mean, I am sorry but..."

"Spit it out, boy."

Justin felt terrible,

"I might be late again tomorrow, sir. And maybe the next day too, I don't know."

"What are you talking about?"

"I'm to be a page for Lord Athelstan, sir."

"Says who?"

"Sir James, sir."

"Is Sir James in charge of the choristers?"

Justin started trembling,

"No sir, but I must go."

"Why should you be permitted to stay in the choir school if you are not a functioning member of the choir? This puts me in a very difficult situation."

"I... I'm sorry, sir, but I..."

Master Rickson dismissed him with a grunt of frustration,

"We will have rethink this arrangement. I will speak to you later."

Justin hastily made an exit with his eyes lowered and feeling utterly helpless. He desperately wanted to be a page but he did not want to miss rehearsals and services either. Even if Master Rickson allowed him time away from the cathedral he would always consider him to be unreliable and a nuisance and he would never be accepted by the other boys. But did he have a choice? He could not refuse the orders of the lord of the province, even if he had wanted to.

Justin was so engaged in his dilemma that he almost tripped over Arthur who was sitting in the shelter of the cloisters. He looked frighteningly pale and Justin instantly forgot his troubles and knelt down next to his friend,

"Arthur, are you alright?"

"I just feel very tired," said Arthur in a weak voice, "and my head hurts. I didn't sleep well last night. I'll just... I'll just stay here for while."

"No Arthur, I think you are ill. You mustn't stay out in the cold. You should go to bed."

"I'm too tired," murmured Arthur gazing vacantly at Justin through closing eyes.

Justin pulled him to his feet and half led, half carried him towards the choir school. Arthur clutched him with feeble hands and stumbled every second step. It took them some time to reach the dormitory and, by the time Arthur had collapsed onto his bed, it was clear that he was suffering from more than fatigue. Justin loosened Arthur's collar, took off his shoes and pulled the covers over him. He then dashed downstairs to find Matron, who was washing up in the kitchen,

"Matron, there's something wrong with Arthur. I think he must be ill."

Matron instantly followed Justin to the dormitory and approached the bed. She looked at him for a moment, then felt his brow and put a hand on his chest. After a moment she said bluntly,

"He has a fever. I'll take him to the sick room. Tell all the boys to stay away from him."

With that she lifted Arthur as if he weighed less than a dry leaf and carried him out of the room. Justin stared after them helplessly. He wanted to help, but what could he do? After tidying Arthur's shoes away, Justin dropped to his knees beside the bed. He was about to clench his hands and send up a prayer when Jonathan walked into the room and stared blankly at Justin for a moment then asked flatly,

"What's the matter with you?"

"Arthur has a fever," answered Justin with a slight tremor in his voice.

Jonathan looked at him for a while, without expressing any emotion, then walked out of the room.

Justin shut his eyes tightly and prayed,

"Dear God, please help Arthur get better. I think you want me to be here, but I need you to know that I'm not strong enough to stay here on my own; I really need Arthur to help me. But since you are God you probably know that already. So please, I want to be strong and I'll give anything I have, but please don't take Arthur away. Please God. In nomine Patris, Filii et Spiritus Sancti. Amen."

He spoke as loudly and clearly as he could. He did not want there to be any risk of God not hearing his prayer.

The sick room was a little room underneath the stairs without a window. Matron was back in the kitchen and Justin crept down the stairs and into the cramped infirmary. A candle burned faintly on an upturned barrel and a bucket of cold water stood beside it. Arthur had a damp, rolled-up cloth on his forehead and he lay on the small bed looking deathly pale. Justin knelt beside him and stared at his friend. Arthur looked weak and fragile, as if a gust of wind might blow him away at any moment. His breathing was quick, his pulse was racing and his skin was burning hot.

Justin dipped the cloth in the water again, wrung it out and replaced it on Arthur's brow, speaking softly as he did so,

"You are going to be fine, Arthur. I said a prayer for you. You will feel better soon."

Then he left the room quietly.

That night Matron told all the boys not to go near the sick room. They nodded absently: they had seen this before; it was a fact of life at the cathedral choir school. If anyone was going to get ill they could have guessed it would be Arthur Smyth: he had always been the runt of the litter. The only question was: would he survive?

Chapter 8

The next morning, after Matins, Sir James arrived for Justin,

"Lord Athelstan will see you now. Quick as you can. Is that as presentable as you can make yourself? Well, it will have to do."

Sir James took the boy's hand and led him through the streets as before. Justin was too old to be led by the hand really, but he did not resent it. He could guess that it was some sort of ancient formality that he was part of and, besides, the touch of this gentle man's hand was calming and gave him the comfort he desperately needed. On arrival at the keep, Lady Winters helped him to change into his pageboy outfit with swift efficiency, and it became clear that they really were expecting him to see Lord Athelstan today. From the weaving room, they walked through the great hall to the stairs that led to the second level. They then swept through corridors lined with shining swords, shields and suits of armour. Tall men in chain mail frequently tramped past them, bowing respectfully to Sir James and ignoring Justin. Eventually they arrived at an ornate, studded door. Sir James prepared to knock, but he suddenly withdrew his hand, turned to Justin and said quietly,

"Now listen carefully, young man. You must only speak if his lordship addresses you directly, in which case you must answer 'yes, my lord' and nothing further. Do you understand?"

Justin nodded and his heart started to race. Sir James smiled down at him then knocked firmly on the door three times. In response, came a clear, baritone voice,

"Enter."

Sir James lifted the latch and gently guided Justin into the room. He gazed curiously at the new surroundings; it was a medium sized room with a high roof and a large fire providing the light and warmth that the shuttered windows might have provided during summer months. On the far wall hung the unmistakable tapestry of Lord Athelstan, which Justin had seen being created at the monastery and, sitting directly below it at a table strewn with documents, was the man himself. He was not overly tall, but he was broad-shouldered and very powerfully built. Though his rough-shaven face had not yet lost all of its youthful appearance, a cynical wisdom shone from his dark eyes. He stood up as they entered,

"Ah, Sir James, welcome. Shall I have the servants bring a tankard of wine?"

"Thank you my Lord, but I will not stay. I was just delivering your new page, the country boy."

"Ah yes," said Lord Athelstan sitting down with a dry laugh. "Lady Winters seems to think he will 'calm my troubled mind'. If he is a military genius and has 10,000 knights at his back he might yet."

Sir James directed Justin towards the table and spoke gently but with authority,

"Please my lord, let the boy sing you a song. Lady Winters and I are concerned for your health; something sweet and calming will help your mind to focus."

The lord sighed and brushed the dark hair from his eyes,

"Thank you for your concern, Sir James," he said sincerely, "perhaps the boy will help me, clearly nothing else will."

Sir James stooped respectfully and left, leaving page and lord alone in the big, empty room. Lord Athelstan continued his work for a few minutes and Justin stood staring curiously at the powerful man sitting before him. Eventually, Lord Athelstan replaced his quill and returned the inquisitive gaze,

"So, you sing?" he asked bluntly.

Justin was fascinated by this man and his nerves where forgotten as he answered rapidly,

"Yes, I sing in the cathedral and I used to sing in the chapel at home, but I was trained in the monastery, I'm still a probationer, but I'm learning quickly and..."

Justin stopped, suddenly remembering that he was not meant to say more than 'yes, my lord'. Lord Athelstan reacted by laughing loudly,

"Typical country boy: no manners but no fear!"

"Why should I be afraid?" asked Justin with genuine curiosity.

Lord Athelstan stared at Justin, highly amused. He held up his rough, strong hands with a half-smile,

"Do you know how many armed men these hands have slain?"

"Quite a lot, I think," answered Justin eagerly, "Brother Patrick told me you have a hand of iron for your enemies, but a hand of compassion for your subjects."

The ironic smile faded from the man's face. He looked at his hands for a moment then asked quietly,

"What else did this Brother Patrick tell you?"

"Not much, but all the Brothers say that you are a good man, so I don't think I need to be afraid."

"Fascinating," said Lord Athelstan thoughtfully. "If only everyone believed it. I am not very popular with many people in the city."

"But I know lots of people who like you," said Justin eagerly.

"It is not a question of being liked. It is a question of whether my stubborn morality is in the best interests of the province. Since we are about to be annihilated, I do not have much of a case and there are some, with a good deal of power, who seek to remind me of it daily."

At that moment there was the sound of a loud, deep voice from the hall.

"Here is the worst of them now," sighed Lord Athelstan. "Excuse me one moment."

A tall, muscular man threw back the doors and entered. Justin immediately recognised him as Earl Guy and inadvertently moved to Lord Athelstan's side. The lord stood up politely,

"Earl Guy, a not-so-unexpected pleasure. Wine?"

"Save the formalities Athelstan, you know why I've come."

"I can think of several possible reasons, enlighten me as to which one."

The Earl strode purposefully towards the table,

"The time for small talk is over, Athelstan. Your foolish pride is going to be the death of this province. You know as well as I do that the barons are on the move."

Lord Athelstan remained standing and spoke in a warning tone,

"If you have come to attempt what your last four assassins failed to do, I suggest we step outside immediately."

The earl folded his mailed arms, looking at Lord Athelstan through narrowed eyes,

"Quite an accusation Athelstan and quite a challenge. But I have no need; I will be lord one way or the other. My concern is in minimising casualties and ensuring there is something left of my province once your misplaced piety has led you to the gallows."

Lord Athelstan leaned forward very slightly,

"Need I remind you, earl, that you are not lord yet and I have every right to have you executed for such insubordination. Perhaps you would prefer it if I mobilised the army now and stormed your castle instead of defending the people. It would give me an advantage since, when the invasion begins, you and your knights will, no doubt, be joining the barons in the butchering."

Suddenly, the earl noticed Justin,

"That boy, he humiliated me at the cathedral."

"I like him more and more," said Lord Athelstan with a wry smile.

"Give me the boy and I will leave you in peace."

"He is my page. What do you want him for?" asked Athelstan flatly.

"To take him to my castle and make him scream for what he did to me, if you must know."

The earl moved towards Justin and tried to grab him. Justin clutched Lord Athelstan desperately. The lord spoke calmly without looking at them,

"Leave my page alone. I'm sure he only did what most decent people in this province would have done if they had the nerve."

Earl Guy grabbed a handful of Justin's suit and hauled him bodily away from the table. Suddenly, Lord Athelstan grabbed the earl's arm and held it in a vice-like grip. He whispered with menace,

"Let go of my page and get out of my keep. I am lord of this province and you are trying my patience."

Earl Guy dropped Justin in a heap and departed with a snarl. His footsteps faded along the corridor and Lord Athelstan sat down and returned to work.

Justin was trembling, almost petrified by his ordeal. For a moment he had thought that Lord Athelstan was going to let him be taken and he was now rooted to the spot. After a few moments, Lord Athelstan glanced at his page and, seeing the fear in the boy's eyes, felt a strange need to comfort him. He asked in an unintentionally gruff voice,

"Did the earl hurt you?"

Justin shook his head. There was a long silence. Eventually, Lord Athelstan stood up and lifted Justin onto his leather chair,

"Stay there for a few minutes. You'll be fine."

He then ruffled Justin's hair and walked towards the door.

"Where are you going?" cried Justin in sudden panic.

Lord Athelstan turned round with a half smile,

"To get you a drink. I'll be back in a moment."

"But I'm supposed to be waiting on you," protested Justin.

Lord Athelstan laughed and walked out. Justin sat looking nervously at the door, he breathed a sigh of relief when the lord returned carrying a tankard of wine and a goblet,

"Your drink, my lord!" he chuckled.

"I don't like wine, sir," said Justin apologetically.

"I've mixed it with boiled water. Just have a sip, it will calm you down," said the man pouring a few drops of wine into the goblet.

Justin slowly took the goblet and drank the wine then put it down with a grimace. Lord Athelstan laughed,

"Don't worry, that will help a bit, my boy."

Justin jumped on hearing the term that Father O'Brien used to use for him. It brought back a warm feeling of security that he had not felt since he left the village and he found himself slipping into his old day dream. The man who had rescued him from the barons was now standing in a dark room, but Justin suddenly noticed that there was only blackness where the man's face should have been and he was filled with terror. He tried to turn away but found that he could not. He closed his eyes but he could still see. Then a soft light shone on the man and revealed a kind, compassionate face smiling down on Justin. His fears vanished and he asked 'who are you?' The only answer was the sound of a bell ringing far off...

Justin leapt to his feet,

"Oh no, I'm late for rehearsal."

Lord Athelstan looked up from his work,

"You don't need to worry about that."

"Yes, I do. I'll be whipped if I'm late again."

"Tell them you were waiting on me."

Justin said nothing, but stared imploringly at Lord Athelstan. The lord looked at him for a moment then waved his hand,

"You had better go then. I shall see you tomorrow."

Justin ran as hard as he could but by the time he stumbled into the cathedral the rehearsal was in full swing. He tried to creep into his place, but all the boys simultaneously turned to look and Master Rickson glared at him. The rest of the rehearsal passed uneventfully and Justin tried desperately to make a good impression by singing every note clearly and with perfect pitch. Alas, when it was over Master Rickson turned to Justin and said the dreaded words:

"Come with me, boy."

The moment Justin had followed Master Rickson out of the cathedral, the boys dashed out and ducked behind the cloisters.

"I'll bet my weeks allowance that he cries," said a boy.

The others murmured in agreement and watched as Justin was led into the close and towards the fountain. Master Rickson produced a leather strap.

"I'll take that bet," came a voice from the edge of the cloisters. The boys turned to see who had spoken and saw Jonathan staring vacantly at the scene before them.

Justin trembled as he stood clutching the side of the fountain. He stared into the murky water and saw his pale reflection staring back at him.

He did yet not know whether he was to be given seven or fourteen strokes for his offence, in the horror of the moment his mind was spinning madly. He feverishly whispered 'be strong; be strong' to himself as he waited in agonising anticipation for the first lash.

It hit him just above the knees and he gripped the fountain desperately as a torrent of pain, fear and anger rushed through his body. How he survived the next six he did not know, the pain and the shock somehow merged into one as he struggled to remain standing. He dared not look round to discover if he was due more, he hoped and prayed that he was not: he could not bear even one more. Just when he was sure it was over, the next seven came:

Thwack!

Thwack!

Thwack!

Thwack!

Thwack!

Thwack!

Thwack!

Then it was over. Slowly, the world started turning again and the emotional and physical numbness turned into real, burning pain. He stood by the fountain, gasping for breath for several minutes, but he did not cry. The shock was still controlling his body, however a calm determination was controlling his mind. He felt the eyes of the boys watching him and he knew, for now, that he simply had to be strong. After another few minutes, he stumbled back to the choir school.

Once inside, Justin knew he had to forget his pain and visit his friend; he went straight to the sick room to see Arthur. His own troubles were forgotten the moment he saw him. Arthur was as pale as death, though his skin was burning hot and his eyes were red and feverish. Justin knew that he was slipping away, he dropped to his knees beside the bed and clasped Arthur's hand. He prayed out loud with a quavering voice,

"Dear God, please don't take Arthur away. I'll give anything, anything at all; and I don't care about being strong now, I just want Arthur to get better. Please... please..."

"It doesn't work," said a voice from behind him. "If He does exist then He doesn't care."

Justin turned to see Jonathan standing in the doorway. There was no hint of irony or sarcasm in his voice,

"I tried it. I tried and tried, and I begged Him and I cried all night but He didn't listen. My brother still died. I'm sorry, Justin."

Justin was too shocked and choked with emotion to speak. Eventually, he managed to stutter,

"It's not your fault."

Jonathan remained in the doorway,

"It's not just Arthur I'm sorry about," he said with a tremor in his voice. "Don't you know why I hated you so much when you came? I was jealous. You were so talented even though you hadn't had proper training and you could have beaten me in a fight if you'd wanted and you weren't afraid of anything even though you were just a probationer. Then you were chosen to be a page for Lord Athelstan and even my own mother loves you more than she loves me. You're honest and brave and strong and I'm just an envious failure."

Justin tried to digest what had just happened. Amid all his pain and grief, it became suddenly clear to him how it must feel to be someone like Jonathan; someone who had to rely on their achievements and talents to have any sense of self-worth; someone who did not realise that they were loved unconditionally.

Emotion was flowing through Justin like a raging torrent and he knew that any moment it would overwhelm him. Jonathan; Arthur; Master Rickson; Lord Athelstan; Earl Guy: faces flashed through Justin's mind with a hundred different connotations. He pushed past Jonathan and out of the room. He didn't know where he was going; he just had to get out. A hot, muffled cloud filled his head and the tears that he had held back for weeks began to well up in his eyes as he stumbled out of the choir school... and straight into the arms of a tall man in the doorway.

Justin had always had someone to hold him steady when life became too hard to bear alone. Somehow, it seemed natural that the arms he had fallen into should be those of Father O'Brien. He clutched his mentor tightly and did not question why he should be there. Then came the tears; warm, heavy tears of deep emotion flowing shamelessly from the boy's eyes. Father O'Brien held him in silence for several minutes. Neither of them felt the need to speak or any embarrassment, even if the whole world had been watching them they would not have cared. Eventually, Father O'Brien looked at Justin and smiled,

"Well, I don't suppose there is much point in asking you how you are getting on!"

Justin smiled. Nothing was too much to bear now that Father O'Brien was here. He turned up his tear-stained face and looked the old monk directly in the eye,

"Father, I need to ask you something, but you have to promise that you won't just tell me that I'll understand when I'm older or anything like that."

"I promise," said Father O'Brien seriously.

"Well it's just all those things about being a healing wind and a light in a dark place and all that. I need to know what it actually means. I want to give what I have but I don't know how to do it."

Father O'Brien paused for a few moments, then he breathed out slowly and said,

"Well, where should I start? The first thing you need to realise is that you are a beautiful boy on the inside as well as the outside. Your company can give great pleasure to people and when their thoughts are dark and malicious, you can change them just by being there. That's what I meant by being a light in a dark place. Does that make sense?"

"I suppose so."

"And as for the healing wind. Well I just thought it was the best way of describing what it is like for someone when they have been plagued by fear and doubt and someone like you comes along and brings joy into their lives in the first time. I knew that you were going to a very dark and toxic place, but I also knew that you were strong enough to fight all obstacles, though I'm sure it has been hard for you."

Justin rubbed the tears from his eyes,

"Why couldn't you have explained what you meant before I left?"

Father O'Brien stroked the boy's hair affectionately,

"Because it is not something that you must do, it is simply about being the wonderful person that you are. That was the only thing I could say that would make any sense to you."

"What can I do to make my friend better? He's dying of fever."

There was a long silence. Father O'Brien sighed,

"You can only give what you have, my boy, and you do not have power over life and death. Sometimes God says 'no' when we ask for something and we must trust that He knows best."

Justin controlled himself, staring imploringly at the monk,

"Will you at least look at him, and see if you can make him better?"

"Of course I will," said Father O'Brien.

Justin led the way to the sick room where the door was still slightly ajar. Outside, Jonathan was sitting with his head in his hands and sobbing violently.

"That's Jonathan Winters, the head chorister," said Justin quietly. He could not think of anything else to say. He found no pleasure in the distress of his former tormentor; in fact he felt only pity, and when Father O'Brien stooped down to speak to the boy he did not feel envious.

"Hello Jonathan," said Father O'Brien gently. "Do you remember me? I'm a friend of your mother and of Sir James."

Jonathan jerked his head up, shocked and embarrassed,

"I... I'm sorry, sir," he spluttered, avoiding eye contact and wiping his eyes brusquely with the back of his hand.

"What for? There is nothing wrong with letting your emotions out before they get the better of you," said Father O'Brien with a quick smile at Justin. "Why are you crying?"

Jonathan stared straight ahead, wide-eyed,

"Arthur is dead."

Justin dashed into the room and to the bedside. Arthur's skin was cold and he was lying completely still. Justin backed out of the room with trembling limbs and sat down next to Jonathan in complete shock. Father O'Brien stooped into the room and the two boys were left alone, united by their pain.

After a few minutes Father O'Brien looked round the door and smiled warmly at them,

"Arthur is not dead, my boys. The fever broke."

Chapter 9

Soon the rumours were confirmed: Prince Edward, the son of King Henry the Third, had escaped from captivity, raised an army of loyalists and was marching towards the city. Meanwhile, the Baron's Alliance was gathering its full strength and preparing to invade the province. Father O'Brien had arrived at the city with a host of cavalry recruited from the fighting monks of his Order and they rode out with Lord Athelstan's knights in a pre-emptive attack against the barons. The cavalry attacked at dawn and routed the troops of Montfort's son at Kenilworth, forcing him to retreat to the nearest stronghold and allowing Edward's army to make preparations to meet the main army of the Baron's Alliance in battle.

Lord Athelstan toasted the first victory with Sir James in his keep. Justin waited on them, his sword hanging ceremoniously at his side.

"Word has it that Earl Guy and his knights have fled the province," said Lord Athelstan filling his goblet.

"Yes, my lord," said Sir James. "Prince Edward and his army will be arriving tonight and border scouts are on the way to tell us the whereabouts of Montfort."

"He will, no doubt, still be trying to unite with what is left of his son's army," mused Lord Athelstan leaning over a map. "His only option is to pass by or through the city. He cannot leave it any longer: all of England will soon know that the loyalists are fighting back at last."

"And what of the king?"

"We can only assume that he is still held captive and is with Montfort's army. Either way, our only hope of freeing him lies in defeating the Baron's Alliance tomorrow."

At that moment, the doors swung open and a border scout dashed into the room and bowed to Lord Athelstan,

"Montfort has crossed the border in the southeast, my lord. His army has occupied the town of Evesham."

Lord Athelstan suddenly turned a deathly pale,

"Muster the army," he rasped "we march immediately."

The scout looked for confirmation of this order to Sir James who shook his head and dismissed him with a wave of his hand. Lord Athelstan glared at Sir James as the scout departed,

"How dare you defy me!" He pointed at Justin. "You boy, saddle my horse now."

Sir James moved between Justin and the door,

"My lord, what is this madness?" he shouted. "Prince Edward arrives tonight and tomorrow we will march out and crush the Baron's Alliance. What possible reason can there be for throwing away the advantage that we have awaited for so long with this rash action?"

"I will go myself!" yelled Lord Athelstan moving towards the door. Sir James blocked his path. The lord tried to push past him,

"Out of my way you old fool!"

"Pull yourself together," shouted Sir James, desperately, and struck Lord Athelstan across the face.

There was a stunned silence. Eventually, Lord Athelstan moved away and sat back in his chair. After a few moments of staring at the table he said quietly,

"I am so sorry. Please forgive me, Sir James."

He sat motionless for several minutes and Justin and Sir James could only look on in bewilderment. Lord Athelstan wrestled with a barrage of emotions as his memory swept through the years of fighting and selfless striving that had brought him to this moment. He thought of the personal sacrifices he had made and the people he had neglected as he followed his difficult and painful path. Eventually the lord raised his head,

"Earl Guy is gone and tomorrow the power of the barons will be dissolved, there is no reason why I must keep my secret any longer. Both of you sit down and listen to the story of a broken man."

They obeyed silently and with intense curiosity. Lord Athelstan sighed a long laboured sigh then spoke gently,

"For the last five years of old Lord Athelstan's life I served him as part of his personal bodyguard. He was impressed with, in his own words, my grasp of military strategy, my moral ideals and my fearless leadership qualities. Against all the recommendations of his advisors, he insisted that I should inherit the province on his death as he had no living children. The likes of Earl Guy saw this as a direct insult — that someone younger than they with no rank or fortune should be chosen above them — but the old lord was insistent. I believe he had foreseen the trouble ahead. He saw to it that I was inaugurated and surrounded by loyal friends such as you, Sir James, and Sir Winters and his good wife and family."

His voice became stronger and a passion blazed from his eyes,

"It was only when our lord had passed away, that I realised fully how much he was relying on me to hold together a desperate province. How

I wished he had chosen someone else. All I wanted to do was go home. To go home to... my wife and child... yes, I have a family. Their existence had to remain entirely secret or the likes of Earl Guy would have certainly used them to blackmail me in unthinkable ways. If I were to be killed, my son would have been in real danger from the barons as he is next in line. But I knew that if I weakened for a moment the barons would immediately take over and turn the province against the king. I had to remain as hard as stone and a man without feelings. For nearly eight years I have been living with the knowledge that I have deserted my beautiful wife; that my son is growing up and that I am missing it all. Now at last there is a hope that my family and I might live in safety and yet, alas: of all the insignificant towns that the Baron's Alliance chooses to occupy it must be Evesham. For my wife and child still live in a nearby village: my home."

Sir James shook his head slowly as he pondered this revelation,

"Does anyone else know of your family, my lord?"

"No-one. Lady Winters suspects, I believe. My wife knows where I am and she understands. I know she does."

"They may be safe, my lord. Montfort was a man of chivalry. Surely he will not allow his men to pillage unrestrained."

Lord Athelstan clenched his fists,

"Do not underestimate what desperate men will do; I must expect the worst for now."

Justin stared at Lord Athelstan. A powerful feeling that he could not ignore was welling up inside him. It was like a day dream, but it was becoming more and more real every second. This was no dream, not this time. It had to be true; somehow, he knew that it was true. A question burned on the tip of Justin's tongue. As if detecting it, the two men turned towards the boy. Justin looked the lord in the eye and said in a breathless voice,

"Are you my father?"

Lord Athelstan's eyes suddenly widened as he stared at the boy, as if really seeing him for the first time, he gasped and stood up. Then, with grim determination, he approached Justin and briefly examined the birthmark on his left shoulder. The two then stared at each other in silence. Lord Athelstan broke the gaze, turning away with a cry of astonishment,

"What a fool! How could I be so..."

He stopped himself, took a deep breath and turned round again to face Justin. He touched the boy with trembling hands and said in a voice that quavered with emotion,

"I'm so sorry. I'm so sorry, my son..." He chanted almost feverishly, "my son, my son, my son, my son..."

Justin looked at the humbled lord with a curious expression, not sure how to react. A glance at Sir James assured him that he ought to say something, so he knelt down on one knee and said in a clear voice,

"I forgive you, my lord, for whatever it is that you are sorry for," then as an afterthought, "am I allowed to say that?"

Sir James burst into nervous laughter and Lord Athelstan hugged his son with tears of joy flowing from his dark eyes. He whispered a prayer of gratitude as he embraced the child that he had loved from afar for almost eight years.

Justin felt whole now and realised very suddenly how much he had missed this man. Somehow, he felt no resentment or awkwardness in the reunion, only a warm contentment as he considered what a wonderful thing it was to be loved by a father.

Chapter 10

Prince Edward arrived that night with a considerable army and the following morning the combined forces were assembling outside the keep and spilling into the streets. The army was to be split into three with the intention of surrounding Montfort and outflanking him. Justin peeked into the great hall where the generals were being informed of the strategy by Earl Gilbert de Clare and Prince Edward himself. Justin studied the face of the prince with intense curiosity. Edward looked every inch like the fearsome warrior that he had imagined from the descriptions and the desire for revenge burned in his sharp eyes. The loyalists seemed to be in no doubt that they would win the battle, a solemn confidence radiated from every soldier and commander, and it filled the city with a strange, passionate energy.

Justin dashed out into the courtyard as the generals dispersed. His father soon emerged and ruffled his son's hair playfully,

"This is the day, Justin," he smiled, "all our waiting and suffering has not been in vain. When I return, I promise to be the father that you deserve."

"But I'm coming too," said Justin, grasping his father's hand and staring up at him eagerly, "I can ride, and I can fight too."

Lord Athelstan looked down at his son for a moment, then said thoughtfully,

"I suppose this is the part where I should tell you that it is too dangerous and that you must stay here where it is safe. But what would your mother want? She wanted you to be safe, of course she did, but in the end she let you take a risk so that you could be with me. Perhaps I should honour that courage."

He started to walk down the steps from the keep, followed by Sir James and Justin,

"My cavalry will be covering the rear of the army as a mobile reserve," Lord Athelstan said loudly. "If you wish, you may ride with us, and if you want to watch the battle from a distance I will not stop you. You will be safe enough if you use your common sense."

Justin nodded enthusiastically, swelling with pride at his father's faith in him. Lord Athelstan then approached the nearest stableboy and told him to saddle a good horse for his son. Justin dashed to the cathedral to say goodbye to his friends.

Lord Athelstan watched his son disappear down the street. Sir James pulled urgently on the lord's arm,

"What are you doing, my lord," he asked in an urgent whisper.

Lord Athelstan did not avert his gaze,

"Letting my son see what no child should see. If I fall today, he will be lord of this province and he must learn that war, for all its glory, must be avoided at all costs. When he sees the massacre he will understand."

He turned to Sir James,

"Besides, after the battle, we must search the town and villages to find my wife, and, if she is dead, I will need my son as much as he will need me at that moment."

As Justin arrived in the close he saw Jonathan and Arthur, now fully recovered, coming out of the choir school. He shouted and they ran towards him gleefully,

"Justin! Are you coming to sing evensong tonight?" enquired Jonathan breathlessly.

Justin shook his head gravely,

"I'm going to war," he said.

"Are you going to fight?" asked Arthur with wide eyes. "Matron told us that Lord Athelstan is your father. A baker's boy told her that the barons are going to be defeated so it doesn't need to be a secret anymore, I think the whole city knows already! Is it your father who is making you go to battle?"

"He's not making me, I want to go. I want to see the action and I want to stay with my father and, when it is all over, I'll go and see my mother too."

"But... but what if..." stammered Arthur, "what if you get hurt... or even..." he trailed off.

"He'll be alright!" said Jonathan with gusto, then, eying Justin's sword, "say, Justin, do you know how to use one of those?"

Justin drew the sword with a flourish,

"You bet I do, and it's sharp now. I whetted it last night." Justin sheathed his sword and became serious, "but I just came to say goodbye. You know, just in case."

"Goodbye Justin," said Jonathan giving him a hug. "You know, you changed the choir. It was like everyone was secretly frightened of each other before you came. It's different now: better."

"You're the bravest!" said Arthur hugging Justin too. "I'm so glad you came."

Justin gazed around the close. How strange it was to compare this moment to the day when he had first arrived at the cathedral, full of nerves and apprehension; when he had clutched Father O'Brien and prayed that he would be strong enough to stay; when had he felt, for the first time, the true meaning of loneliness. So much had happened since then, things he could never have imagined, and now here he was again wondering what the future had in store for him. But there was a trusting innocence in Justin that no amount of bitter suffering, loneliness or war could break; a simple faith that glowed from his young heart and touched everyone who knew him. At last, he understood: the 'shining light' and the 'healing wind' were not about doing or even giving something, they were about being someone, and all he had to do was remain true to that person.

"How strange," said Justin quietly.

"What's strange?" asked Arthur.

"Just everything," smiled Justin.

The army had already started to pour into the city streets as Justin dodged back up the road to the keep. Every corner was filled with the clink of metal, the shouting of orders and the bray of horses. Lord Athelstan was leading Samson into the courtyard as his son arrived. A stableboy led a feisty pony out to stand beside the lord, who then effortlessly lifted Justin into the saddle,

"There you go, my boy. Now use your common sense. If the fighting gets too close, turn round and keep galloping until you get back to the city. Some of my best men will meet you at the gate."

Justin turned in his saddle,

"Are we going to win the battle, father?"

Lord Athelstan threw back his head and laughed recklessly. He looked at the boy and said with an intense sparkle in his eyes,

"Yes Justin, we are going to win the battle!"

The noise of marching and the smell of horses filled the air as the army marched along the road towards Evesham. Justin was sure that the ground was trembling with the beat of so many hooves and feet, the sound was almost deafening. As they neared Evesham, a few shouted orders were passed along the line and the army began to split into three divisions. Prince Edward took the centre column and, as they pushed onward, they hoisted the banners of Montfort's son to lure the baron's army out of the town.

They trotted over the brow of the hill and Justin suddenly recognised the Vale of Evesham. Though he could not see it, he knew that the town was not more than two miles ahead.

"Halt!" shouted Lord Athelstan to his cavalry, standing up in his stirrups. "We cover the rear from here. Every man keep a watch to see that Montfort does not try to outflank us with his cavalry but ride only at my command."

The column led by Earl Gilbert de Clare passed by them and assembled to the rear of Edward on the right flank, hidden by the brow of the hill. When the army was in position, the hillside seemed to be full of a tense expectation. A dark cloud started to spread itself across the sky and a cold wind began to spit rain into the faces of the soldiers. Every man stared grimly at the horizon for the banners that would inevitably appear soon now. Several minutes passed and it grew darker. Then came the distant sound, almost imperceptible, but unmistakable nonetheless: the marching of a host of mailed feet far below. Next the banners appeared, and then the army of the Baron's Alliance pricked the skyline.

Justin felt a surge of emotion thumping through him. Hot and urgent; fear and excitement mixed together, filling his mind and body. It was thrilling and terrifying all at once and his heart beat painfully against his chest. He sat transfixed by the sight of the seething mass that was pouring up the hill and growing larger all the time. The horses beside him were stamping and tossing their heads restlessly and the soldiers, though silent, were no less determined. Prince Edward sat proudly on his warhorse displaying no hint of emotion.

Suddenly, the Baron's Alliance broke into a charge with a mighty cry that shook the hill. Justin saw the army forming into a wedge shape before his eyes and coming closer by the moment. Still Edward did not move and Justin felt sure that his heart was about to leap out of his chest with the suspense. Montfort's army was almost upon them now and Justin could see the faces of the men in the front line as they charged towards him. Prince Edward raised his arm, then let it fall again and immediately the arrows from three hundred longbows filled the darkening sky. Before the first volley had found its mark, a second was on its way. Several of the attacking soldiers tumbled to the ground, and in the next few moments the armies clashed.

The sound was one that Justin knew would remain forever engraved in his mind: the cries and screams of hundreds of men losing limbs and lives. It grew louder and more frequent as the momentum of the charge carried the Baron's Alliance far into Edward's column. The deafening horror made Justin want to close his eyes and cover his ears, but he was transfixed, unable to move. He could only wish with all his might that it would end soon.

Edward's soldiers started to waver under the ferocity of the attack, yet Earl de Clare, instead of reinforcing Edward, started to move his column steadily down the hill. Edward's men were being pushed further and further back and some had already retreated. Justin looked, perplexed, at his father, while Lord Athelstan stared ahead, motionless. Earl de Clare's column kept marching until they were almost behind Montfort's men then, suddenly, they turned and, with a blood curdling cry of 'for the king', plunged into the rear of Montfort's army. At the same moment, the third division attacked the flank and the entire loyalist army let out the deafening war cry:

"For the king!"

By this time, the rain had begun to fall heavily and it was becoming harder to see. The Baron's Alliance was completely encircled and they desperately formed a defensive ring for all round protection. The loyalists hemmed them ever tighter in and it seemed that every man was seized with a lust for blood as the Baron's Alliance fell in their hundreds. Some started to throw down their weapons but they were slain regardless.

Another strange feeling gripped Justin, completely unlike anything he had felt before. He knew, deep down, that something was wrong. Not only because the battle had turned into a massacre, but there was something else. Then he saw it, near the edge of the defensive circle there was a soldier on a horse, dressed in the livery of the Baron's Alliance and wearing a helmet with a visor pulled down over his face. He had no weapon and his hands were tied to the saddle. Justin pulled his father's arm and pointed,

"I think that's the king down there," he shouted above the din of battle.

Lord Athelstan stared intensely into the battle throng for a few moments then, suddenly, he spurred his horse down the hill and roared back to his cavalry,

"Protect the king!"

The cavalry assumed it was a war cry and thundered after the lord shouting 'for the king'. Seeing this, Lord Athelstan urged Samson to a dangerous speed in order to reach the fighting first. As he waded through de Clare's soldiers he pointed and shouted desperately,

"Stop, stop! Protect the king!"
But the men were crazed with the heat of battle and did not hear. Lord

Athelstan managed to force his way through to the king and, with a final effort, lunged and tore off the helmet. The soldiers who saw the face revealed instantly stopped fighting, it was indeed the king. Gradually, the message rippled through the army and the fighting died down as the remainder of Montfort's army dropped their weapons and knelt with their hands above their heads. The rain poured down and mingled with the blood of almost four thousand corpses. Montfort had fallen along with most of his knights; even the temptation of large ransoms had not stayed the loyalist's lust for revenge. Years of bitter conflict had made them desperate to ensure that no-one would survive to rise up against their king again. The clear tones of a trumpet fanfare pierced the heavy air as the task of finding the wounded and burying the dead began.

The battle was won and the power of the Baron's Alliance was forever broken.

Lord Athelstan mounted Samson again and galloped back up the hill to his son. He then grabbed Justin's pony and headed towards Evesham. Justin's heart sank as his little village came in sight: it looked as if it had been hit by a hurricane. Every door had been broken down and smoke was rising from some buildings. They cantered through the deserted pathways and up to Justin's house, after swiftly dismounting they dashed into the little cottage.

A sick feeling entered the pit of Justin's stomach. His home was decimated; his mother's loom had been smashed and his own bed was in shreds on the floor. The sight shocked him to the core, more than any battle scene could have done. Lord Athelstan placed a hand on his son's shoulder,

"It is just common pillaging, my boy. She might be alright."

At that moment the clatter of hooves resounded outside. Lord Athelstan drew his sword and stood in the doorway just as Father O'Brien galloped up,

"Good day, my lord," he shouted, reining his horse to a stand-still. "I took the liberty of riding back to Evesham two days ago after our victory at Kenilworth. I have secured the townspeople in the monastery."

"All of them? Is my wife safe?"

Father O'Brien gasped in astonishment, "Your... wife!" He studied the lord's face, "William?"

"Yes, it is me, Father."

Father O'Brien laughed,

"Then get yourself up to the monastery, William. Serena has been waiting for you for almost eight years!"

With joyful laughter, Lord Athelstan hoisted Justin onto Samson then leapt up himself and followed Father O'Brien to the monastery at full gallop. The rain that had seemed so cold and dreary a moment ago, now seemed cool and refreshing. At last, they clattered through the gates of the monastery and into the courtyard where Serena was already waiting.

Lord Athelstan leapt from his war horse as his wife ran to greet him. They embraced passionately as Justin clambered down and ran to join them. The lord was weeping like a child and he held his beloved wife as if he would never let her go again. They stared into each other's eyes, exchanging every thought and feeling that mere words could not express. Serena then stooped and kissed her son who smiled back at her lovingly. She stroked his wet hair as she whispered 'my precious boy' in her gentle voice.

"He saved the king's life," said his father. "How often the fervour of men almost destroys the very thing it seeks to protect. Our son taught me that."

"Our son..." repeated Serena, smiling joyfully at her husband. The man lifted Justin onto his broad shoulder,

"Our son will be the best lord this province has ever had. He is just, he

is fearless and he is strong!"

Justin laughed his carefree, young laugh. Now that his parents were united his joy was complete. They could live together in security for the first time and nothing need tear them apart. Furthermore, his future lay before him: a life of adventures in a world that needed him.

The End